Barb;
It's a start.
More coming
soon!
Jim

7-

DEATH IN SPADES

Jim Speirs

INKWATER PRESS

PORTLAND • OREGON
INKWATERPRESS.COM

www.inkwaterpress.com

ISBN-13 978-1-59299-349-9
ISBN-10 1-59299-349-4

Publisher: Inkwater Press

Printed in the U.S.A.
All paper is acid free and meets all ANSI standards for archival quality paper.

DEATH IN SPADES

JULY, 1967

The firing began to quicken. He knew that time was measured in seconds now. Adrenaline pumped. He thought the wound wasn't bad. The leg was bleeding but the bone was spared. Voices, the high-pitched sing-song noise of the Vietnamese, could be heard clearly now, behind the fallen Marine. He was low in the grass. The bullets of the AK-47s cracked around him. Rounds passed over his head, through the brush, close enough to tell him that the gooks knew where he was, and in seconds they'd pinpoint his exact position. Then and there he would die.

For once, he was happy to be small. A little man makes a harder target. It was a nice thought, and for the moment it struck him as funny. All his life, he'd wanted to be bigger. A large man, maybe a football player. Heavy muscles, a commanding presence, one that demanded attention. Maybe a swimmer, long, lean, narrow waist. All the relatives would marvel at his size and how much he'd grown over the last six months. Girls would covet him. He could choose who to date. He'd be popular. He'd be handsome. Maybe get laid by some homecoming queen. But now he was thanking his God for being a near runt. *Make me smaller*, he pleaded, silently, for anyone to hear. *Make me the size of an ant. Let me become one with the dirt. God, let me dig; just this once, give me mythical power to disappear into the ground. Make me smaller.*

Mark Rose reached for the hole in his thigh. The sun beat on him with a ferociousness that defied description. The sky was not blue, but rather a silver-gray color that burned his eyes with salty water and made the simple act of breathing a scorching agony. It was as if the sun and sky were together as confederates with the hunting Viet Cong. The world was closing in on him, each element in vicious harmony with his extinction. The exit wound had left a gouge in the rear of his leg. He could feel the opening. Big enough to put his fist in, with pieces of flesh dangling as the blood pumped out. He reached for a compress, something to stop the bleeding. The bullet passed over his knuckles, blasting the medical kit from his grip and leaving white bone exposed where seconds before a complete hand had been. More rounds followed, his eyes filling with sweat, dirt, and filth. There were more voices now, and they were much closer. Moving in for the kill, the smell of death in the air.

He buried his face in the ground, the loose-powdered red earth filling his nose and mouth. The noise was becoming deafening. How could they be shooting so much? Why hadn't they killed him yet? He coughed. Soil seemed to come from his lungs. I can't fight all of you. Not the earth. Not the sky. Not the sun. Not the dirt. Not all these gooks. Where's the rest of the squad? If I can just hang on for a few minutes more they'll come and I'll be saved. Rescued and medivaced home. A wounded hero. Just a few more minutes.

Desperate measures were required now. The Vietnamese must have started fires in the grass to his left. Smoke blinded him, and the heat from the scorching sun and burning land made the short Marine realize two things. One, that the forces combined to kill him were taking on a form of their own. Life was being pumped into the elements: the sky was beginning to breathe, the earth was opening its eyes, and the Viet Cong had enlisted the grass to follow the orders of Ho Chi Minh. As their life grew, his faded. Secondarily, the gooks must have lost sight of him. The fire was meant to flush him out. The dinks didn't know he'd been hit. Hell, I couldn't run if

I wanted to. My leg has a four-inch hole in it. The fire had been set to force him to run, make him an easy target. The gooks had lost him in the tall dry grass, but he could hear the voices, and each voice seemed to be aiming at him. They had to know, the burning grass would soon tell on him. *Viet Cong grass,* he thought. *I'll be killed by Viet Cong grass.*

The Marine Lance Corporal rolled to his right, away from the grass. *Don't let me burn to death. Where's my squad?* Twelve Marines were no more than sixty yards behind him. He'd been the point man. They had to be close. *Marines fight to the death for fellow Marines,* he thought. Twelve men. All the firing, some of the rounds must be from his saviors, fighting their way to his rescue. He couldn't be sure...maybe the enemy force was larger than he thought. Maybe the whole squad was cut off. Feelings went through him in milliseconds. Mark Rose felt his torso twist, as his mind tried to leave his body. Trying to separate the two, the Lance Corporal was left with the split-second distinction that forced the recognition of shock and horror. *This can't be happening,* he repeated, *this must be some bastardized dream.* Bullets whizzed by, each one seeming to look for him, sinister little copper projectiles that cracked as they passed. Did they have eyes, like the distorted cartoon figures from animations of his youth? Like the sky above him, they too seemed to have life. Eyes that sought him out. Each round knew his hiding place, each one smelled him. Each one told the next bullet where to look. The smell of burning grass was mixed with cordite, and all he could think of was the blast furnace that was his caldron of death. A ring of fire that conspired with all the foreign elements to insure his gruesome earthly departure. The sky was on fire. Twelve other Marines were his only hope. Where were they? Could they be blocked...cut off from his position by a V.C. force that had set up to interdict the Marine squad? *Semper Fidelis.*

As he reached a small berm, the slight Marine could nearly feel the Viet Cong troops opposite him. They couldn't be more than twenty yards away. Smoke blew over him just as he inhaled, causing

3

him to cough and giving away his position. The smoke was so thick now that the Viet Cong pursuers were having as much trouble as he was. He had no choice; the coughing was sure to bring a quick response from the killers. What he couldn't have known was that the cacophony and confusion were so great that nothing short of firing his weapon could have given up his whereabouts. He didn't know. Over the top of the small hill he heard voices. For the first time, his wounded leg throbbed. His mouth and throat were dry. Scorched. His stomach tried to escape through his anus. Death was near. The firing began to grow faster. Urgency of dying. *A few shots. If I can get in a few shots, kill a few gooks, at least I'll have an even score. They'll kill me, but not before I take two...maybe three of them with me. Fuck it, I'm going to die anyway.*

Crawling to the top of the two-foot-high slope, Rose peered across the smoking landscape. A branch next to a three-foot-high ant hill gave him more cover than he'd expected. God of Israel, thank you. The Star of David dangled in the dirt beneath his chest. Two Viet Cong soldiers appeared almost casually to his front. *Well, this is it. Shit, I've only been in this damn country nine weeks, fired some shots but probably never hit a thing. So now there are two dinks right in front of me, I'm going to die anyway, so let me take these bastards to the great cosmic consciousness. This is what I came to do, a Marine, a trained killer—departure is so close, I'm beyond fear, just resigned.*

He raised his M-16. The black plastic wand of death zeroed in on the two Vietnamese soldiers. At twenty yards, the little Marine couldn't miss. Center shots, the torso would dissolve, hydrostatic shock setting internal organs to mush. Laying the rifle on the dirt, the bleeding Marine calmly got his sight picture on the Vietnamese chest. *Well, we're all gonna die...so you go first.* The Viet Cong was standing now, a perfect target. Fish in a barrel. He'd get off five, maybe eight shots; then all the gooks in the area would have his number, but the score would always be in the small Marine's favor: *two or three of you to one of me!* The bastard was smiling! The Viet Cong soldier actually seemed to be grinning. As the sweat poured from his brow, he placed his mangled hand on the forward stock. Thoughts turned to his fellow Marines, and to why he hadn't heard any noise from the distinctive report of their M-16 rifles. Where were they? Did he accidentally get further ahead of them than he thought? How far was the separation? Did he really screw up, and was he completely cut off? *Close*, he begged to his God, *they must be close...coming to save me.* The terror, the fire, the confusion, all this combined to obfuscate the whereabouts of his fellow warriors.

A deep breath. It caused his leg to pulse. *Steady, hold the picture.* Thick clouds of smoke rolled past the end of his rifle barrel. The Viet Cong's death was but seconds away. Shots continued to fly in all directions, eyes searching, looking for the little Jew. Squeezing the trigger, the small man waited for the .223 round to fly at 3100 feet per second. The Viet Cong foot soldier had less than a second to live. His laughing buddy was next. Wouldn't know what hit him. *Fucking dinks!* Now, the man would die. *You rice-eating gook, you're about to leave this planet!*

Snap. The Jewish Marine looked astonished at the weapon that is every Marine's primary tool. The rifle and the Marine. One and the same. No matter what your job description as a Marine, you were always a rifleman first. Lance Corporal Rose had qualified as a "Sharpshooter" at Parris Island, so the unexpecting V. C. directly in front of him would be an easy kill. The man next to him wouldn't have time to react before Rose shot him also. Legends. Marine phantoms of wars gone by were seated on his M-16. He pulled the trigger. Ghosts of men who had preceded him seemed to guide his last few actions. Click! Nothing. Panic. Smoke, dust, blood, and a failed attempt to kill a man were what he was left with. He pulled the rifle back from the firing position and looked incredulously at the weapon. Full magazine, twenty rounds, easy charging handle, no jams. *What the fuck?* He pulled back the bolt mechanism to see what could be wrong. Nothing. Bullets flew close to him, they mocked him: "We're shooting, and you're not, and you're going to die!" Up to the top of the hill again, the Viet Cong were still there, unaware of their closeness to death. Chamber a round, get the sight picture, and kill the man. Click! Gooks saw the movement.

Why didn't the weapon fire? Too much time had elapsed, there was no answer. Click, click, click. Nothing. The gook heads turn. They've found him, and his end is near. Hand and arm signals from the Vietnamese pointed the way to the wounded Marine. Gooks didn't know if, or how badly, the Jewish Marine was hurt. They circle and close. The sweating Marine frantically looked to his rifle. What was wrong? Nothing to see. Dink voices are close; now they're spraying the area, to flush out the Marine. A Chi-com grenade flies close, the explosion concussing the man's brain. Smoke is thick, shadows move as the day draws to a close. The M-16 doesn't work, and the little man seeks the solace of the dirt. An AK-47 round finds its mark; the Marine is hit in the buttocks, thrown in the air and falls on his back. Shock is complete, and the man now comes to realize how much blood he's lost as the killers tighten the circle.

Sensing that there would be no resistance, the V. C. close. Nearly twenty men of the Viet Cong killing unit rush their hapless prey. The Jew prays and asks the God of Israel for forgiveness. A 7.62 X 39MM AK-47 round rips into his hip. The shock blows the Marine into a fetal position as the broken rifle he depended on flies six feet from his gravesite. Another grenade explodes and peppers the helpless Marine's body with pieces of odd-shaped steel. The bleeding is not as furious as it could be; much of the body's blood had been lost to the ten-minute-old leg wound, and the white hot metal has cauterized the grenade damage. The Marine is losing consciousness, all is gone. He sees the first soldier crest the hill, firing on full automatic. Clouds of smoke confuse the area; even the gooks can't get a clear picture at ten feet. They fire. Seeing rounds creases the forehead of the dying man. He will die, and the outcome of his death will not change the result of the flawed war. The Lance Corporal felt the life flowing from his young body, blood filled his eyes, and a vile taste flowed in his mouth and throat. The wounds left no doubt to his adversaries that he was dead. He lost his sight. Head injuries left massive amounts of blood so that his face was not recognizable. He passed out. Vaguely he recalled the Viet Cong soldiers turning his body, scavenging the would-be dead Marine of all his web gear. Stripping him clean of all his useful items. The Viet Cong soldiers didn't linger. They feared the onset of the Marine squad and, like their contemporaries who'd been fighting the struggle for decades, took what they could. They had less than thirty seconds.

Helicopters were heard in the background. The Viet Cong troops grabbed the M-16 that the young Marine had used to try and defend himself. Standard stuff, they always took the weapons. The body was left for graves registration.

A Viet Cong soldier stopped over the body of the Marine. For twenty years he'd struggled, lost his son, and recently his wife. He hated the Americans. He loathed the bloody body in front of him. He'd lost his humanity; he was a casualty of the war. He knew of the excesses of the Ninth Marines, especially 1/9. He would take a prize. Reaching down, he grabbed the bloody head of the small Jew, and pulling a captured K-bar knife from his belt, held the Marine's head with one hand and sliced off the ear with the other.

Not all that uncommon. Trophies. Ears were the favorite. They were easy, and the level of human degradation was not unique to anyone. Excesses. Things that would not have been considered when a person first entered the war were now acceptable practices after a brief time in this surreal world that was home to thousands of troops on both sides. An ear, tongues, scalps. Penises stuffed in a soldier's mouth—sometimes when he was still alive, so he would suffocate on his own genitals. The Viet Cong troops had had a good day. A dead Marine, an undamaged rifle, ammo, web gear, canteens, and a human ear. A great day, and not one of them had suffered so much as a scratch. Hot and sweating, they retreated into the tangled undergrowth of a hedge line not more than forty yards away. Rotor blades were now distinct; the gooks knew that the gun ships would be strafing the area soon. They disappeared into the dense vegetation.

Dust-caked Marines moved cautiously toward where the point man had been ambushed. Sweat poured into their eyes as the radioman talked to the circling choppers. Slowly, with rifles pointed to the sides of the trail, they trekked along the jungle path. No more than eight feet separated them from the thick, impenetrable forest. Fear welled up in their throats; the jungle was alive, it was the enemy's home. The brush was in league with the Viet Cong. It, too, conspired with the enemy to make each Marine's life one of continued terror. Demons waited as they moved purposely, one step at a time; booby traps could separate limbs from torsos with one wrong move. The jungle could be concealing another Viet Cong ambush. Hundreds of enemy troops could be waiting only a few feet away. The jungle would not tell, and the Marines could not see. Death was close, death had visited, and the short man's life had ended. The advancing Marines were sure of that. With this thought in mind, the Marines were extra careful, and extra slow. What's the use of rushing to the aid of a dead man? Especially a dead man that no one was sorry to see gone. Mark Rose was done with, the Marines knew this without having to look, and not one of them felt anything but relief.

"We see the down man," the medivac pilot said. "He's not moving, but can't tell much more than that. Too much smoke. You guys are about thirty yards out. He's off the trail to the left."

"Roger that," the radioman replied, "are you taking any fire?"

"Negative, the gooks must have di-di'd out of here. Gonna have the ships prep that tree line anyway, the bastards probably left some cover."

"OK, keep a crew above us. Hell, the place was crawling with gooks a few minutes ago, and we don't want to lose any more men pulling back a corpse."

The fires were smoldering now, not much flame but plenty of

smoke. Marines coughed and rubbed the thick sweat from their faces. Uniforms that were less than three weeks old had been reduced to tattered rags that hung to their ulcerated limbs like filthy patchwork remnants. Dysentery racked their bodies. Malaria infected many of the men who'd been in Viet Nam as grunts for over five months, causing alternating cold chills and indescribable fevers. Weird bumps developed on the Marines' bodies, appearing one week and disappearing the next. Rashes were chronic. Their crotches, red and infected, would crack and bleed, toenails fell off and teeth were loose. The land itself would kill you. Now they closed in on the dead Marine as the smoke scorched their lungs. Lungs that should have been young and healthy but were now infected, damaged, and diseased. The men, caked with the debris of a thousand napalm strikes and the residue of the Agent Orange powder that coated the land, spit huge wads of indescribable green-ish-blue phlegm.

Eyes darted left and right as the lead Marine moved to where the chopper was circling overhead, telling them they'd find their fallen comrade. Watch the tree line. Watch the jungle trail. Watch for booby traps. Watch for the little man's body. "Where the fuck is he?" the nervous Marine cried to himself.

He nearly tripped over the bloodied body. "God," he thought to himself, "if that'd been a gook, I'd be dead, fuck."

Using hand and arm signals, he motioned the other Marines to his side. "Spread out, set up some cover," he bellowed, as the Marines moved to create a temporary perimeter just like they'd done so many times before. "Give me the radio, let's get the dust off down. Doc, get up here, get the tags off the fucking Jew, and let's get the hell out of here!"

The corpsman ran in a crouch to the squad leader, not bother-ing to unsnap his medical pouch. The man was dead, and his job was to confirm it and get the twisted corpse on the helicopter. He slid to the side of the prone Marine, silently noting the massive amount of blood that surrounded him. Automatically, he reached to the man's throat; he was trained to do that, test for a pulse, any sign of life. Fingers moved through the slippery gore feeling for something he was sure did not exist. After eight months as a Navy Corpsman assigned to a Marine infantry unit, the medical man knew death.

"Hurry up, Doc, tag him and bag him," the squad leader yelled. "All this smoke, every fucking gook in three klicks gonna be here soon. Shit, we might just as well send them written invitations, fuckin' dead Jew's gonna be the death of us all. Hurry, man!"

"I gotta pulse!" the corpsman screamed. "Gimme water, for God's sake, the man's alive...he's breathing, I've got life here!" The medical man frantically tore into his bag, looking for tourniquets and a syringe.

"Get over here, for Christ's sake. I need a syringe and a god-damn bladder! Morphine, I need my other bag, gimme the shit!"

Time stands still now, everything goes into slow motion, people and events in half speed. Mouths open, voices cannot be heard, Marines point and the elements close in. Seconds become minutes, and minutes an eternity. Unknown eyes observe the scene as moments blend, and the innocence of youth takes a quantum and immediate leap to old age. All of the elements combine to mock their frailty, as one man's life becomes the microcosm of an entire war. As the realization of what's occurring sinks in, the Marines of the ragged squad look at each other with perplexed yet knowing eyes. Something's gone desperately wrong. People's futures stand in the balance, as each man knows what's at stake.

"Get the choppers down now, right away," the corpsman demands as he injects the second vile of morphine. "Gunther, get over here and help me with this plasma, goddamn it. Get on the horn and get those birds down!"

As in a dream sequence, the mechanisms necessary to respond to urgency assume a pace that seems as if the participants were running through waist-deep water...stress and slowness. A Marine has the handset to his mouth. He looks to the sky as he speaks.

The circling helicopter seems stuck in place as it rotates in a three-hundred-sixty-degree arch. The pilot is nearly certain that ground fire will soon rack the ship. A gook ambush, medivac one man, bring the chopper in, and all hell breaks loose. The chopper starts its drop, two hundred yards of airspace that can turn lethal in a fraction of a second.

On the ground, a Marine races toward the medical man. Once upon him, he snarls, "Doc, fuck this dead Jew, we can come back for the corpse later, this is gonna get hot again! Fucking gooks are close, probably more of them too. Let this asshole go, we gotta pull back and get a perimeter, let the ships rake the area, call in some arty. We'll come back later, I'm calling off the choppers!"

"Fuck you, Gunther, this man's alive! He sure as hell won't be for long. Leave him here? What the fuck are you thinking? Some Goddamn Marine you are, now get that ship down here, I'm not going anywhere until this guy's on his way out! Dead or alive!"

The helicopter hovers two feet off the jungle floor. The corpsman orders Marines to grab the wounded man's arms and legs and lift him onto the craft. The Marines look at one another and don't move. Instead, they stare back at the frantic medical man as he races with time to save a man's life. Some of the Marines curse openly as they cast their eyes at the drama being played out in the tall grass.

"Help me, for God's sake!" the corpsman hollers. "What the hell is going on here?"

Reluctantly, several of the closest Marines come to the aid of the corpsman. The battered body is lifted onto the waiting chopper, and within seconds the craft is hundreds of feet in the air, headed toward the medical huts of Dong Ha. If the man lives, he'll be moved to the better-equipped facilities of Danang, and from there Japan, and eventually the States. If he lives.

"OK, form up and let's get the hell out of here," Gunther barks. "Every fucking dink in ten miles gotta know where we're at. We're moving about two klicks west, there's a few good hills to set up on for tonight. We need to move fast, I want to be dug in early, get our coordinates to arty. Shit, we're too deep in Indian country. Move out!" The squad leader glares at the corpsman as they pass.

Filthy, ragged, sweat-drenched Marines formed up and moved single file toward the west, nearing the base of the Annamese mountains. An evil place, full of mystery, ghosts, unknown creatures and primitive peoples. This would be their home for the night. The point man moves out, and the others follow.

"I want to talk to you," the corpsman said to Gunther.

"Talk all you want, Doc, but do it when we get to the hill and we're dug in. I'm in charge of these men, and your young ass, and I don't need any more dead people today!"

"Rose ain't dead!" Wood shot back.

"Well, he will be, probably is already—shit he was hurt bad, I know a dead man when I see one. Believe me Doc, all you did by wasting your time on that Jewish cocksucker was to put the rest of us in more shit. Now, I'm done talking, get a move on, and if you want to cry about some dead bastard, we can do it later. Now shut up and move!"

The Marines got to the hills an hour and a half later. It was a fast, exhausting hump, and the men still had to dig fighting holes.

Night was approaching as the haunting mists had begun to swirl out of primeval valleys that cut deep into the mountain range. Insects began their assault on the tired Marines as they raced with time to dig their holes a little deeper. The damp earth stunk of decay and rot, and the fading light prevented the men from seeing what type of crawling worms were awakened, or if their digging might disturb the snakes. The terror that each night brought to Viet Nam was nearly on them. The elephant would soon be standing on their chest, the fear and pressure compressing their lives with unspeakable demonic monsters.

Doc Wood stepped up to Gunther. "I want an explanation," he demanded.

"Of what?"

"You know what. Don't play stupid! What the fuck went on back there? What happened to Rose?"

"Jesus, are you one dumb ass, Doc. How long you been in country now? Do I have to draw you a picture?" Gunther drawled out the sentence and sighed.

"Now bullshit, Gunther, just because you're a fucking sergeant and been in the Nam longer than me doesn't mean I'm a fucking idiot! What happened?"

"Stupid green pea Jew got out further than he should and got sapped. How goddamn hard is that to figure? End of story. Happens all the time. Now get your ass in your hole, I gotta call in our position or you'll have a bunch more work to do before the night's out! The gooks gotta know where we're at—shit, half the valley probably saw us set up—now cut the crap and dig a hole. I gotta get the pig guns set up for some decent fire coordinates."

"Sergeant Gunther, I'm not finished!"

"Well, I am, so maybe when we get back to regiment you can talk to the chaplain, he might give a shit. I sure don't. Now, I'm giving you an order: make the rounds, and get in your hole, I got lots of shit to do."

"Why didn't anyone help him? Why?" The compressed face revealed a new angle, and the squad leader knew he would have to answer. All part of the job, he thought to himself.

"Listen, you silly bastard," Gunther screamed. "Nobody liked him. Nobody! And if by some freak of nature he lives, nobody's gonna like you either! You best hope he dies, or is fucking medivaced to the moon! He was trouble, a sissy little New York Yid, everyone knew he was gonna get someone killed. He just didn't fit. I ain't gonna spend a lot of time explaining specifics, but enough of my men are seasoned veterans to know a pile of shit when they see it. And he was shit! Rose was going to get good Marines killed, and he had to go! Period! Now, is that clear enough for you? If you ain't figured, this is a grunt unit. We're here to kill people. Rose shoulda been some Remington Ranger back at Pendleton or some other shit. He didn't fit with the grunts, and my men would have had to carry his ass all over Viet Nam. He got left there for the good of the squad—Christ, for the good of the Marine Corps! We did the right thing: he's gone, we're alive, and you're gonna keep your mouth shut! Understand?"

Doc Wood looked into Gunther's eyes. They were blank and flat. Like looking into the bottom of an abyss. There would be no rationalizing with Gunther, he had crossed over, the demons of Viet Nam had him, and there was no returning.

"I understand you killed one of your own men, Gunther. That's all I understand. You should be proud!"

"Fuck you, Doc. First off, I didn't kill him, the gooks did. Second, we all knew it had to happen, wasn't no one gonna go up and risk his ass to save some Jew who should have stayed at Harvard or some damn place. Now forget about it, it's over and we got a bad shit in front of us. The beast is out tonight, and he's hungry."

A full ten seconds passed as the two stared at each other. Doc Wood turned and left, and as he walked away, he could feel the cold eyes of Gunther on his back. In the hot, humid, tropical night he felt a damp fear crawl up his spine, like a dozen earthworms were inside his shirt. This was not his world, he'd just been told of a murder. He was here to save lives, not bare mute witness to his fellow American soldiers' deaths by execution. He also knew his place in the squad, and that there were many ways to die in Viet Nam. The worms seemed to cause an uncontrollable shiver as they moved across his shoulders.

A half hour passed. Sunset had turned to purple, then the Viet Nam night closed, and the world became black. A blackness known only to the blind. Monsters appeared in a land where everything was foreign, and the swirling mists took on a life of their own. In the distance, tracer rounds could be seen. Green projectiles from the Viet Cong AK-47s, red from the American M-16s and M-14s. Green chasing red. Red returning the favor. Mortar tubes belched, a flicker of light, then went out. From the middle of the impenetrable sky came a waterfall of red. Silent in the night, "Spooky," the C-130 gun ship, was doing his work. A beautiful wall of orange-red death fell from the heavens as the corpsman tried to sort out his day. After five minutes of hard thought that only left him more confused, a noise interrupted his concentration.

From behind, a Marine crawled next to Doc Wood's hole.

"Doc, I heard you and Gunther. I just want you to know... someone to know, that I didn't want to go along with it. Not everyone was in on it. I thought it was wrong, but hell, what was I gonna do? Get myself killed? For what? It was wrong, man. But shit, this is the Nam, and I'm pretty new here. I just pretended not to care, and hell, it's over, and nobody coulda stopped it. I never touched his rifle."

"What do you mean, his rifle?" Wood replied.

"You didn't know?" the voice asked. Their speech was muted; they were no more than two feet apart, but still Wood could not see a face. Viet Nam blackness.

"Know what?" Wood said. "I know that nobody tried to save Rose, he was left out there to die. That's all I need to know."

"You need to know this, too," the anonymous voice said, cutting the night and sending shafts into the medicine man's soul. "Rose didn't have no firing pin—they took it out the fucking night before. While he was off shift, they fucked with his rifle. I heard they took the pin, but I'm not sure of that. All I know is that they messed with it to make sure it wouldn't fire. He was off watch, probably 0200 hours or there about; he was sound asleep...didn't know shit. They hated him, poor bastard. Never had much of a chance anyway, but shit, with a fucking 16 and no firing pin, or a bent pin, what the hell was he supposed to do? Don't answer, I'll tell you—he was marked to die, and that's what happened."

"Are you sure? Jesus, that's unbelievable."

"Yeah, I'm sure, I saw it with my own eyes. But who's to say now? Rose is dead, and the dinks got his weapon, and none of these fuckers gives a shit. I mean, who's gonna talk, and where

would you get any proof? Shit, this is the Nam, and what happened today is already another lifetime away. But still, I wanted
you to know, it's only right. Some of the men messed with his
rifle...Gunther knew it...hell, he might have ordered it."

"Rose wasn't dead when he got on the bird," the Doc replied,
"but he was plenty screwed up, and probably didn't even make it
to Dong Ha—too much blood, too many holes. Shit! No firing
pin? Are you sure? Jesus, what did he ever do to deserve that?
What's your name?"

"Doesn't matter," the voice said, as it retreated into the inky
night, "just wanted someone else to know. And I had no part in
it, really. I guess being a little smart-ass Jew was deserving enough.
I don't know, none of my business." The fading sound reiterated.
Then there was silence. In the distance, a flare illuminated the sky,
just enough light to outline the back of the anonymous Marine as
he disappeared into a ghostly darkness. The parachute flare swayed,
flickered, and went out. The black terror of the impenetrable night
returned, and all concentration was riveted to the immediate need
to stay alive through the coming hours of darkness.

JANUARY 1999

As usual, it had been a beautiful day in San Diego. It had been a good day for Danny Miller also. At fifty years of age, Danny had led a truly charmed life. A successful broker at a local commodities house, he only regretted that he hadn't been chosen for the company promotions he felt he more than deserved. Driving to his favorite bar he pondered the changes that had taken place along I-15 as he cruised toward Rancho Bernardo and his first gin and tonic. The air was fresh, breezes off Point Loma had made southern California Danny's only home for the last twenty-six years. He loved it.

The house he'd purchased twelve years ago was easily worth twice what he'd paid. His three children were less trouble than many of his friends' kids; although Danny suspected his son of continued cocaine use, he closed his eyes, and felt sure he would outgrow it—after all, Danny had known a few excesses in his life also. His health was holding, and although his wife had confronted him about women more than once, he'd never been caught.

Danny missed the last fling. The redhead. She'd been so nasty, so willing. And the hair was legit...the carpet matched the drapes. He wondered if the reputation of hot-blooded redheads was real, or if he'd just been lucky. He thought of her and all the unnatural acts she loved to perform. He thought of her as he pretended to make love to his wife. *Probably a good thing she moved away*, he pondered, as he turned off the northbound freeway, but the stirring in his crotch made him lust for the unmentionable. So pretty. So young. And, lord was she a pervert! What a great life, and who knows, tonight might just be the night he'd meet her replacement. He checked his wallet, snug in his sport coat, removed his wedding ring, and looked in the mirror, brushing his hair just right so as to cover the five-month-old hair plugs. Friday night. He told his wife not to wait up...you know, "company business." He paid the bills, and she didn't have to work—hell, she shouldn't complain, just a night with the boys. And if it got too late, too many gins, well it was a twenty-minute taxi ride home. *I've got it made*, he thought, as he marveled at the lush landscape of the beautiful San Diego countryside. Mostly, he loved the broad-leaf ferns. They always relaxed him, even after all these years.

He recognized a few faces at the bar as soon as he entered. No names, just faces. Probably better that way, he thought; if he should get lucky, at least no one knows your name. Danny checked his watch—it was close to eight o'clock. The night was young.

By nine thirty Danny had finished his fourth gin and tonic, and he was feeling excited. Fluid, loose and relaxed, he looked in the mirror and convinced himself that he had far fewer wrinkles than his contemporaries. The lighting was perfect for this charade, the drinks, the darkened recesses, *Hell,* he kidded himself, *I don't look a day over thirty-five.*

Small talk resulted in nothing, and by ten thirty he was ready to move on. This time he figured he'd be a bit more daring, head out east. No place in particular, just drive toward the desert and the cowboy bars that were part of the landscape. Nothing wrong with a cowgirl, but he'd have to be careful—Friday night, and the long stretches of rural road would be crawling with highway patrol cars. He turned the radio on, searching the dial for his favorite "oldies" station. A flood of memories washed over him as the Rascals sang "Groovin'" and he sped into the warm California evening.

Before he knew it, he was on the outskirts of Lakeside. Not really his kind of area, but still it offered plenty of challenges. The land was sparser here, and much of the decorative gardening included huge cactus. He pulled his car into the parking lot of Spanky's. It was well lit with a giant neon cowboy over the entrance. He picked the furthest corner of the lot. Music could be heard from thirty yards away, and for a moment Danny regretted being dressed in his casual work clothes. Tight-fitting Wranglers seemed the norm, especially on the women. As he went through the door, he first thought there was too much smoke. *There's too much smoke and it'll be a dead giveaway to my wife.*

It was evident to Danny after his initial beer that an evening at Spanky's was not going to work. First, he was too late, the locals had hours of drinking under their belts, and although Danny had a good buzz going, he knew he couldn't catch up, so he quickly finished beer number two, and headed for the door.

Good thing I parked at the far end of the parking lot, Danny thought to himself. Give me a chance to air out my clothes. He opened his sport jacket and fanned the desert night hoping to catch the fragrance of honeysuckle in his wardrobe. He stumbled briefly, and quickly stopped and looked around. Cops could be watching people leaving the bar, and if they saw him staggering around from one of their hiding places he would be totally screwed. *Can't afford a drunk-driving ticket at my age.*

His car was in the darkened recesses of the lot. He'd paid no attention to any other vehicles as he'd driven in, and felt relieved when he was able to find the door lock on his first attempt. Rolling the window down, he made a decision to get the hell out of there. This just wasn't going to be his night. He was too far from home, it was too late, he was too drunk and, all of a sudden, he was just too far out of place.

Danny hardly noticed the light crunching sound of loose gravel as he fumbled for the ignition opening. He sensed that he was not alone and turned to see a form that he recognized as human, but in the darkness he could make out nothing else. It was a split second, but seemed like eternity. Slow motion. Danny knew it was bad. He didn't know how bad.

When the bullets that ended his life smashed through his skull and scrambled his brains, he hadn't had time to think, let alone react.

It was not quite four in the morning when Detective Richard Hand woke up. Instinctively, he knew what the call would be about. At thirty-three years of age, he'd been a homicide detective for five years. He'd been lucky, for most cops don't become detectives without at least fifteen years on the force. But the all-hours phone calls of a detective made him wonder if he shouldn't apply for a transfer back to uniforms and a regular life.

"Hand here," he answered, automatically moving from the bed and shielding Brenda, his wife of ten years, from further interruption.

"Dick, this is Jaffe, sorry to wake you, but we've got a problem and the captain says you're the man." Detective Lou Jaffe had transferred to the San Diego Police Department from Houston. He hadn't wanted to, but a messy divorce and plenty of bad memories prompted the move six years earlier. It didn't take much time for Jaffe to recognize that the lateral switch he'd made from Texas was the best thing he could have done. He loved San Diego, and he had had the enviable luck to pair up with Detective Hand as his meteoric career began its upswing. He'd worked with Dick Hand almost since his first day of duty as a San Diego policeman. Like others in the department, Jaffe had quickly learned to respect Hand. He seemed to possess a sixth sense about his work, and his deductive thought patterns were becoming something nearly mythical in San Diego. Hand was a kind of whiz kid who observed situations and quietly made mental notes that confounded some of his peers; he solved seemingly hopeless puzzles, putting them in tidy, logical packages. Jaffe worked well with Hand and intuitively knew that his star would rise or fall with his partner. Jaffe had never asked him what it was like growing up with the name Dick Hand. He could only imagine.

"Well, shit, what's so important that we have to run it now? Don't tell me, Border Patrol's shot another illegal and they want us to make it all better before the paper gets there. Right?" By now, Hand was in the kitchen fumbling to start coffee. No sense trying to go back to bed, his day was beginning a little early.

"No, got a killing in Lakeside, don't know much else, but the boss wants us on it, so the damn thing's probably unsolvable. I doubt we'll know anything else 'til we get there. I'll pick you up in about twenty minutes. I don't know why they always call me first on deals like this? I mean you're the senior officer here, but I guess they want me to be the one to wake you up, want me to take the heat. But remember, don't blame the messenger...I'm just carrying out orders, master." Jaffe closed with a mock expression of plantation drawl, "I be at yo house soon masser Dick."

"Lakeside! Shit, Jaffe, that's county stuff. What the hell, don't we have enough of our own business? This is just great, get me out of bed to do some county mountie's job while they get their fucking beauty rest! Christ, what the hell can be so important that they can't use their own men? I smell a rat, and I think we're just handy. This is a set-up, goddamn it, it's four fifteen, I'm already pissed, my blood pressure is through the roof, my wife will be more pissed, my dog's barking, any second now my neighbor will be woken up by the damn mutt, he'll be pissed. I hate the sissy bastard anyway, and I'll really be pissed to see his faggot face at four fifteen!"

"Well," Jaffe slowly replied, "let's go take a look at the Lakeside corpse before you turn your neighbor into one. I mean, what's the point, you've got a lifetime to make enemies out of folks who live fifty feet from you, and we're wasting time."

There was a long pause followed by low laughter from Dick

Hand. "Right you are, and hell, you're just following orders, so I guess I'll let everyone off the hook and see what the day brings."

It was nearly an hour before the pair of detectives approached Lakeside. The sun had begun its ascent, revealing the beautiful cactus and huge boulders that were part of the east county landscape. Hand wondered to himself, as he often did, what the area must have been like a hundred and fifty years earlier. He could almost see the Spaniards. He couldn't help but think of the Zorro re-runs that were a part of his youth. Dashing men who rode the mesa, singing boleros, winning darkly beautiful women, and being a law unto themselves. Maybe that was it...this was still part of the wild wild west to Detective Hand. He'd read that Tom Mix, a cowboy star of the silent movies, had an adobe house built somewhere near Lakeside. Maybe the attraction of romantic times of yore had been as compelling to Mix as it was to Detective Hand.

Spanky's was on the right. Three police cars from the county could clearly be seen in the morning light. The scene looked typical: yellow tape, men with weapons at their sides, coffee cups on the hoods of the patrol vehicles. The cool air reminded the officers that they were in the desert.

"What a pleasure to see you again," Hand mocked, as he took the county man's grasp, "where's the beef?"

"Over here, in the car," the green-uniformed officer scoffed. "Bang, bang, you're dead. That's all."

Jaffe and Hand walked to the sedan and peered into a front seat covered with blood, a dead man slumped sideways to the right, his hair matted to the skull, and the smell of death permeating from the window opening. *Too many cops walking around*, Hand thought to himself. Straightening up, he asked rhetorically to no one and to anyone who could hear, "Witnesses?"

"None," the county investigator said. "The two guys who found him are over there by my car; they're kitchen help and don't know shit. Mexicans."

Hand raised an eyebrow, as if to say, *you brought me here, let me work—I'll figure out who's clean and who's not.* "Evidence?"

"Nothing yet," the man in green replied, "but it's getting light and we'll go over the area thoroughly again in a few minutes. Just bang, you're dead, for now. Want to talk to these two guys?"

Hand felt the urge to slap the county officer. *Such a cavalier prick*, he thought. *Do I want to talk to these guys? Gee, no, Officer, what did you think, we'll just let them walk away and take your word for it! They're clean. Says who? You?*

Sadly, discussion with the two dishwashers told Hand nothing. They'd left at about three fifteen in the morning. That was normal; the last to go after everything was cleaned up. Mexicans. Good workers, who had walked to the car because it looked out of place at that early morning hour. They discovered the mess, and had called the police and their employer. After only a few minutes, Hand was certain he could eliminate them as suspects. No mystery there, just good workers. So now what?

"Who is the dead guy?" Hand asked, as he surveyed the area. He was like an artist beginning to fill in his canvas. "You got an I.D. on him?"

"Yeah, we made him right away," the county man said. "Name's Danny Miller, lives in the city, no warrants, no priors except a D.U.I. eight years ago; job, family, the whole line of bullshit...a U.S. citizen, I guess. Haven't contacted his family yet, thought I'd let you do that."

"Thanks, asshole," Hand shot back.

Two more hours passed before the preliminary work was done. Lab techs, measurements, print dusting, ambulance, and finally the car was towed to the police impound yard. Dick Hand performed the unpleasant task of informing Danny Miller's wife that he would not be coming home.

A week had passed since Danny Miller died. Dick Hand was feeling the pressure. He was the officer in charge of a case with no motive, no clues, no witnesses, no leads, and a Captain of Detectives with no patience. On top of that, Hand had a reputation to defend. Jaffe and Hand had put nearly a hundred hours into the investigation already. This was Hand's method of work. All cases stood a better chance of resolution if the detective work was immediate. The longer it took, the colder the trail became. Speed and velocity were key and the partners had put virtually all their other work on the back burner. Still, they had nothing. Captain John Del Vecci wanted a daily progress report, and with each passing hour his glares became more dismissive.

"So bizarre," Jaffe said, as they turned off the light and chalked up another fourteen-hour day, "that's the last call we have on the list, and they don't know shit. Hell, we may as well start with 'A' in the white pages and work our way through. We've got nothing!"

"No, it's here...somewhere...somewhere in all this mess is the key, it always is, we just haven't stumbled on it yet," Hand snorted. "Let's give it a night, come in early and sober, and go through it again." He didn't believe his own words, but that's all they had to work with, and he knew the captain would be calling them in soon, so there was no real choice. They'd have to go over all the facts they had and come up with another angle. They would not be permitted to tell Captain Del Vecci that they were at a dead end.

On the way home, Hand tried to reconstruct what they'd learned. Thinking to himself that the solitude of his car was the only place he'd be able to focus, he deliberately took the long, slow route. "Square one," he said aloud to himself.

A dead man. Danny Miller. Father, husband who sometimes cheated on his wife, good worker, stable, no known enemies. And the dead man had had no problems with any of the people at Spanky's that night. Sat, talked, drank, joked, and then left the planet. Why?

Miller's death was no accident, that's all that was certain. In fact, it was so clean, Hand suspected a professional was involved. But he could make no connection, and because of the circumstance, kept the idea to himself. His first instinct was to look at Miller's client list. After all, Miller was a commodities broker, dealt with other people's money. Maybe he'd stolen some, maybe he'd lost big. That was the logical assumption, but the trail went nowhere. Miller didn't carry large accounts, he was a mid-level manager...at best, and any potential problem clients had been checked. That left Hand with nothing, but still, when you mix money into the equation there's liable to be a smoking gun. He'd look again, but for now the thinking was distracting his driving.

A beer—maybe a quiet bar and a cold beer. Dick Hand knew he could come up with another angle under the right conditions. That's what he was known for, oblique theories and ideas nobody else thought of...ideas that solved cases. The drive wasn't working, and he was close enough to home to not be concerned about drinking and driving. He knew the spot, a quiet bar not more than a mile from his house.

After his second draft of ale, he again went over all the random variables. He found himself making notes on the bar napkin. Granted, Danny Miller was out of his territory in Lakeside. No reason to be there, and, as far as Hand knew, he hadn't planned to meet anyone. So, here's Miller in a cowboy bar having drinks late in the evening. Why in Lakeside? The napkin was filling.

Miller.

Lakeside.

Commodities broker.

Old girlfriends?

Sickness? Miller's doctor and an autopsy had ruled that out.

Old enemies? Certainly no killers among them, and virtually every one of Miller's associates over the last twenty years had been questioned. All had legitimate alibis.

Well liked. Danny Miller was a likable guy, funny and sometimes goofy.

Mental? Nothing there. Miller's wife said he sometimes still had terrible nightmares, memories of a young Marine in Viet Nam.

He never shared his experiences with her. The long, faded scar on his stomach was evidence enough to speak ten thousand words. But there was no treatment for any type of mental disorder, and the Veterans Administration had no record of Miller ever needing any medical or psychological help.

Mistaken identity? This, thought Hand, was where they should be looking. A specific hit that went bad...on the wrong guy. The killing was too good to be the work of an amateur.

Another napkin. More notes.

Let's move to the crime scene.

The county cops had screwed things up by the time he'd arrived, that much was a given. Too many people walking through the crime area, but still, what remained remarkable was the lack of evidence.

No shell casing. Two shots fired from a .22, that much was confirmed. The lab determined the killing gun was an automatic. Where were the spent cartridges? No one heard any noise. Someone should have heard something. Even a .22 caliber round, on a quiet, clear night outside of a bar, is going to have a muzzle report. No noise, no casings, no fingerprints. *A pro*, Detective Hand nodded to himself.

No blood trail. No droppings from the assassin as he left Miller's car. Clean and professional. But why Miller? Real pros don't make identity mistakes. Certainly Miller had no connection with organized crime. All mob informers were quick to distance themselves from this one. The small-time gangsters in the San Diego underworld made it clear that the Miller killing had nothing to do with any of their people. It all added up to nothing. Variables. Somewhere in the mosaic were answers, but for Dick Hand, after over two weeks of searching, there were only two things for certain.

One, the killer had a distinct limp. The loose gravel of Spanky's parking lot revealed that much. He'd dragged his left leg from his car to Miller's and back again. *I'm dealing with something different,* Hand thought to himself. *But even that could be fake. A ruse to throw me off. But I doubt it.* The man was slight, the space between steps suggested the murderer was not over five feet four, and he had a real limp, wouldn't be able to move quickly.

The missing ear was the kicker! Miller's left ear had been cleanly severed. Odd type of prize, and certainly a thing that few trained assassins would attempt. Too messy, and too much time involved. Miller's ear had been cut with a surgeon's precision, with a blade so sharp even the coroner had marveled at the good work.

Hand put down his pen and folded the napkins. Suddenly he was tired, and knowing what the morning would bring, opted for the comfort of his bed.

The press had had a field day. The captain was on his ass, and tomorrow he'd have to tell the brass at homicide that the vaunted super sense he'd so carefully cultivated had resulted in nothing. No breaks. No leads. No new ideas. Mercifully, Detective Hand had planned a four-day vacation and, after tomorrow's meeting, he knew he'd need the breather.

That night, Hand dreamed about the ear. An anxious, fitful sleep left him feeling like a picture out of focus when the alarm went off. Brenda gave him distance; she could tell that the pace of the investigation was weighing on him. It had been over a week since they'd had any type of sex, and for this charged couple, that was evidence enough of the strain Dick Hand was experiencing. Brenda was three years younger than Hand. Dark and vibrant, she'd always respected her husband's passion for policing, but subconsciously shared his concern for the danger of the job. Maybe that's why the discussion of children was becoming less frequent. SDPD had produced more than one widow, and the thought of raising a fatherless child held little appeal for Brenda. For now, she simply made small talk about their upcoming mini-vacation.

The morning meeting went worse than expected. Detectives Hand and Jaffe endured both routine and pointed inquiry and insult. Naturally, all those involved had prepared questions that they knew there were no answers for, and it seemed the whole affair was designed to embarrass rather than focus.

"One more crack about Columbo or Kojak and I'll bust," hissed a sweating Jaffe. The meeting had lasted an hour, but it was a long and excruciating sixty minutes that left both men in a high state of anxiety. "So easy for those cocksuckers to sit back and ask shit when they know goddamn good and well there's nothing new... and that smug fat ass from east precinct, how the fuck did he get in there? Who asked him? Fucking El Cajon traffic cop, couldn't chew gum and beat off at the same time, and he's taking shots at us! This is just bullshit, what do you think?"

"I think I'm going away for a few days, four to be exact, and I'm going to try not thinking about this," Hand replied. "I don't need this crap...but they're right in some ways, it is odd that we've got nothing, and we both know that bullshit line we sluffed off on them about having other leads to check out was crap. They saw right through it, and didn't jump in our shit with the who, what, when routine...so count your blessings. Maybe I'll have an epiphany of some sort—the woods do that to me. We're going up to Big Bear. Mid week, so it should be quiet. Anyway, I'll let you know. And if you think of anything—anything at all—let me know. This is how these cases get solved, little inconsequential facts or ideas that don't seem important all add up to solve the puzzle. Believe me...the answer to this killing is right in front of us, we just need to break the code. This is what I think, do you remember when we were in grade school and the teacher asked you to diagram a sentence?" Hand waited.

"Sort of." Jaffe looked confused. "But what's that got to do with this dead guy?"

Hand spoke slowly, "The teacher would put a whole bunch of words up on the blackboard and say to the class, 'This is an incomplete sentence.' You would have to rearrange the words in a certain order...you know, verbs, nouns, adjectives, all that crap...and presto, you'd have a grammatically correct sentence. The point is that the answer to the sentence puzzle was in front of your face, but without the proper order of words, the English language is screwed up and you'd never have a correct or complete sentence. Homicides are like that old sentence in grade school...the answer to the killing has been given to us, we just have to rearrange the clues in the correct sequence and the death will be solved. Easy to say, I know, but the riddle can be solved; all we have to do is reconstruct the items of information in a certain order and we'll crack this case. So, when I say I want you to call me if you have a new idea or angle...call me—it might be the lead that lets us finish the sentence. Get me? Call on the cell if anything comes up."

With that, the two partners went in different directions.

What neither of them knew, or would have had any way of knowing, was the peculiar drama being played out five-hundred miles up the state. Fifty miles south east of Sacramento, police were busy bagging up the two-day-old body of a transient who had died a very violent death. The man had no identification. The typical bum's belongings had been plundered, so there was nothing much left to look at when police covered the scene. A dead man in his late forties to early fifties, if he'd had a wallet it had been stolen, and the authorities were just hurrying to get the job done. After forty-eight hours the corpse was stinking badly, and what the hell...a dead hobo was hardly cause for a county emergency. It was impossible to tell if the same person or persons who had killed the man had plundered his meager belongings or if that had happened later, as other vagrants passed the body. All that was certain was that the man had died of a small-caliber bullet wound to the head.

"Tag him and bag him," the sergeant said. "Send him to Murphy in the deep freeze, get some prints, and the John Doe tags. Probably never know who the poor bastard was, but if there's a God, our man here is in a better place." Mumbling to the two or three men near him, the officer disgustingly stated, "cut off his fucking ear! Jesus, all we have to do is put out an APB on a missing ear! It's kinda funny, really. What do we wire the railroad cops? Be on the alert for tramps carrying a leftover ear in their pocket?"

With that, the unidentified man was loaded into the waiting meat wagon. The next day, the very low-profile death was given a number and assigned a category five. There had been no other deaths of this type in the Sacramento area, and the fact that a bum was dead raised no particular alarm. It ranked just above car thefts and purse snatchings in priorities, and it was felt that the killing would almost certainly solve itself when some hobo spilled his guts after he was arrested for pissing in public. Seemed like it always happened that way.

MAY 1999

The Veterans Hospital in Portland was better than many he'd been in over the last thirty years. Mostly under construction, the new facility was long overdue, but when finished, promised to offer the kind of services that the vets deserved. Large and bustling, it overlooked the Willamette River, and was located adjacent to the prestigious Oregon Health & Science University.

Warmth was making itself known. The long dreary Oregon spring was reluctantly giving way to summer breezes. People were running on jogging paths with determination, trying to make up for the months of winter inactivity. For the disabled man in the rented sedan, the picture this scene presented was certainly of mixed emotion. One was the natural pleasure of experiencing spring and seasonal rebirth. The other, resentment for all those people who walked and jogged so effortlessly while he suffered in constant pain. He increasingly had to move about with the aid of braces or a walker. Now, so far from home, he had to check into this facility. His kidney, or what was left of it, was shutting down, and he needed immediate help.

"Rotten luck," the vet mumbled to himself. He had work to attend to in the Portland area, and the less attention he generated, the better. As he checked in, showing his purple, permanently disabled card, he couldn't help but notice the men wearing the tattered remains of military clothing issued so many years ago. Old jungle fatigues and bush hats adorned the twisted bodies of men he knew instinctively were veterans of Viet Nam. Faded patches announced the various fighting units that had welcomed these men in the prime of their youth. Now scarred and bent, these aging warriors waited stoically for their turn at medical and psychological treatment.

An hour passed.

"Mr. Rose," the overweight orderly called out.

"Here," the small man responded, standing automatically, steadying himself on his cane. He eyed the employee for signs of recognition. He did not offer his hand to the man, who stuck his out for several seconds and then dropped it with a shrug.

"Come with me," the man in the ill-fitting scrub outfit said, motioning to a small, sterile room. "You'll forgive us, Mr. Rose. We're sending for your records, but you're a long way from home, so it's taking some time. I mean, New York is a long walk."

The little man said nothing.

"It shouldn't be too long," the V.A. employee continued. "Your complete medical records are on file, we know that, and we should be getting them faxed any minute. But for now, tell me what brings you to Portland, and what we can do for you today."

"I'm on vacation and I need medication for my kidney," Rose said coldly. "I know the name and dosage of the meds, so we really don't need anything else; if you could get me an attending doctor, I'll be out of here before my records arrive. I don't need a check-up, or physical, just some pills, I'm very familiar with my condition and don't need any special attention. Now, if you could..." The door swung open and a young man whose name tag identified him as an intern appeared with a beaming smile.

"Mr. Rose, I'm Doctor Khali, Ali Khali, how can we be of help?

Your medical records have not arrived—I guess you live on the east coast, right?"

Oh, fucking great, Rose thought to himself, *a goddamn Arab intern. Just what the doctor ordered for a dying Jew, some itinerant towelhead to administer my final meds. Mother of God, this is a mistake. The easy smile and outstretched hand—can't he see I hate him? And I'm not feeling like starting some male bonding thing with some dirty Arab who secretly wishes I were dead. If he only knew how close to granting his wish I was he'd probably fall to his knees, bow to the east, and cum all over his Koran. For now, I've got work to do, and not much time.*

Swallowing, and recognizing he didn't care to cause any unwanted attention, the little Jew decided that he'd do what was necessary to mollify this young doctor. *You attract more bees with honey than shit.*

"Listen Dr. Khali, all I need are some of those kidney pills— I've run out of mine, and I'm on an extended vacation. All this is a matter of record. I've been treated by the V.A. for over thirty years, so I've got the routine pretty much wired. We really don't need to wait for my records; I can give you a quick and detailed description of my condition and disability, so there's no reason to wait for paperwork to figure out what to do. Hell, I've been disabled since 1967, so this shouldn't be a big deal."

Mark Rose did not tell Dr. Ali Khali that he was dying. Did not mention that he knew his life was measured in months. Maybe weeks. Speed was necessary, he needed medication, and he needed to arouse as little attention as possible. *Who's kidding who,* he wondered to himself. *This will probably be my last refill...there isn't much time.* Blood in the urine and the increase of heart palpitations confirmed what he already knew. Death was near. Still he had work to do, unfinished business. A race with time. A race that was almost over. A race that began on a hot July day in 1967.

At the speed of light, memories flashed, and for the moment he was transported through time to that distant valley floor, and as his mind traveled, the decades disappeared. As time warped, and Rose became an involuntary introvert to his own emotion, he was swept to another hospital at another location. Daydreaming, in a trance like solitude, Mark Rose remembered another hospital stay.

JULY 1967

The smell of the smoke was replaced with cool crisp air. Voices could no longer be heard. The numbness of the morphine combined with the noise of the helicopter was the last thing the little Marine remembered. *Dull and sharp,* he thought, as he passed into an uncertain future. *How can the chopper blades be dull and sharp at the same time? What an odd sound. Anthem of Viet Nam.* Then he was gone.

Vague awareness. Comings and goings. That's all the recollection the gravely wounded Marine could remember. Noises, words, pain, bliss, and the gradual realization that he was somewhere very foreign. He floated in and out of the dream. Before he could focus, he could hear, and what he heard made him cringe.

Medical people making comments...comments that he hoped were not directed at himself. After some time, he knew better. He'd died and been resuscitated twice, that much was clear, but after that he was unable to match things together. Maybe it was the drugs. Maybe the wounds. He didn't know. All that was certain was that the injuries he'd received should have killed him, and that for some odd reason he was alive. The attending medical personnel were amazed. Most felt he'd have been much better off had he died. He could hear the conversations, ingest what they were saying, but could neither speak nor see. Inglorious thoughts of his amebic vulnerability crossed his surrealistic condition, but nothing penetrated his cerebral stress except pieces to an unsolved puzzle. Nothing made any sense.

Finally, after what he later learned was a six-week period, images and movements came into view. Hazy at first, but within a few days his vision was restored and he could see the destruction done to his body. He couldn't speak because of the tubes that were inserted down his throat, but what he saw was a mass of bandages. It appeared that only his left foot was not wrapped. The rest of his body was covered in gauze. Doctors responded to his open eyes. They asked questions and he was instructed to answer by squeezing the hand of the physician. One squeeze, yes. Two squeezes, no.

Weeks passed. Tubes were removed, others added. Gradually, a modicum of strength began to return. Blessed with the recuperative powers of youth, the little Marine began to mend. Still, the attending staff at Balboa Naval Hospital informed him that he should plan to remain hospitalized for four to six months. Then look forward to years of therapy. Permanent disability. They held out hope that someday he would even walk. With the aid of crutches. The tube coming out of his penis hurt. Bed sores ached, and bed pans stunk. After six weeks he was able to use his one good hand to reach behind himself and was shocked to learn that the right cheek of his ass was missing!

Flat ass, he thought to himself. *Really, no rear end. At least I'll never be called bubble butt.* He learned of internal injuries, shattered kidney, removed spleen, sections of lifted intestine, broken pelvis, collapsed lung, punctured stomach, and perforated bladder. That was not all. Fingers were missing on his left hand; a deep purple scar ran from his forehead diagonally across his eye socket and down his cheek. The bullet had dug into his upper lip removing a half-inch chunk of flesh before entering his mouth and knocking out four front teeth. His ear had been cut off. Oddly enough, the wounded Marine remembered that event. A blur, for certain, no pain attached, but of all that happened to him that terrible afternoon in the I Corps "Happy Valley," he could remember an enemy soldier cutting off his ear. As he stared at himself in the mirror, all that came to mind were old Frankenstein movies where the tightly wrapped monster terrified hapless humans with his grotesque looks. Women fainting. Children running. And the townspeople forming vigilante parties to slay the beast.

The hospital ward was full of wounded. Men cried in pain all hours of the day and night. Orderlies cursed. Some wounded didn't make it; they died quietly in a morphine-induced coma and were carried out under clean white sheets. Beds were changed and new figures arrived. Young men in the prime of life, their bodies bent and broken, were hauled into the hospital like sacks of flour. The cream of the American crop, Marines who the year before had embraced the immortality of youth and the certainty that they'd never die or suffer serious injury. Now they rolled in agony, as effects of the distant war ravaged their adolescent structures and shattered their youthful dreams, turning them to old men decades before their time. Just as a brick shatters a plate-glass window, the vestiges of youth and innocence blew up and seeped out of this hospital room. Throughout the nation, in hundreds of similar hospital wards, the fading pulse of the Sixties generation was monitored. Petals fell from the flower: peace, love and happiness were never to return. The summer of love had barely blossomed for the face-painted children who frolicked in the hallucinogenic world of universal brotherhood before the blood of their friends spilled onto the floor of their dreams. The dawning of the Age of Aquarius came and went as mothers and fathers wept, and a nation began to question the wisdom of its leaders.

In his third month at Balboa, he was able to experiment with a wheelchair. The excitement of moving on his own surprised the Marine. What freedom. Freedom was fleeting though, as the atrophied muscles of his slight body would not allow him to propel himself over twenty yards; his shoulder strength gave out almost immediately. Healing continued, and by the first week of January, 1968, L/Cpl. Rose was able to stand with the help of a walker for nearly three minutes. By February he'd planned his first step.

February of 1968 also brought a huge, additional number of bodies to San Diego's Balboa Naval Hospital. The lunar New Year had arrived. Tet. The Year of the Monkey, and the carnage was more than the military was prepared to handle. Twisted bodies lined the hallways of hospitals from Japan to Guam, and then traveled to overflow rooms in every state in the union.

Mark Rose was eager to leave Balboa. He'd seen enough, and with the new human wreckage that appeared daily, he was certain that the Navy could use his bed. He traveled the aisles on his walker, trying not to look or to notice the smell of death that gripped every corner of the huge building. He pivoted and started his return trip to his bunk when a face caught his eye. At first, he could put no name to it, but the longer he looked the more certain he was that they'd met before. The man stared straight ahead. He was seated in a wheelchair, disheveled hair, soiled blue hospital gown, and a left leg that went only as far as his knee. Rose slowed and took a closer look. The legless man gave no indication that he knew that L/Cpl. Rose had stopped and was observing him. The shocked hollow eyes of the man gave mute testimony to what he had seen and done. Rose bent forward and read the name tag on the man's chest. *Wood!*

"Doc," Rose exclaimed. "Doc Wood, Jesus, look at you, I can't believe this."

He waited for a response as the man's eyelids flickered, and he bent his head to meet Wood's face. The long vacant look betrayed a whole young world gone mad. Ten seconds lapsed.

"Doc, it's me...Rose, second squad, Bravo Company. Rose, Mark Rose. The little Jew, for Christ's sake." It occurred to Mark Rose that he was smiling, and he couldn't remember the last time he'd done that. It felt like the scar on his upper lip would split wide open.

With that, Doc Wood blinked, and life worked its way into the flat, dead eyes. At that moment there were only two people in the world. Rose reached out instinctively, too fast and too late to remember that he couldn't stand on his own, as he tumbled into Doc Wood's wheelchair. He slid to the floor beside the corpsman's remaining foot. From the floor he looked up, unaware that the fall could have pulled open any number of his delicately healing wounds.

"Rose, you're dead. You had to be, I mean I saw you leave... there's no way, you were way fucked up. I know. This is bullshit... you're dead, so leave me alone, I've got enough trouble. I mean dead men are all over my dreams, I don't need this shit when I'm awake! Now di-di! Di-di mau, get out of here!"

"Doc, I can't di-di, shit, I can't even walk, so I'm stuck. Right here on the floor under your feet until some nurse comes and picks me up, so go figure, I ain't dead, feel me." With that, Rose extended his hand and the two touched, cementing a bond of fidelity that only men of combat could begin to understand.

The two warriors struggled for a moment, but soon found themselves talking in rapid succession, spitting out words in bursts like an M-60 machine gun. An orderly helped Rose to a seat next to Doc Wood, and the two spent the world's fastest hour catching up on old times and events. Most of the questions and answers were not pleasant. The common ground they shared was one of combat, so the subject matter was necessarily grotesque.

"Hey, Doc, you remember 'Ski'?—hell, I never knew his first name. You know, the blond Polack? Guy was always wearing that goofy love bead his girlfriend sent him. Good luck, he said, ward off evil spirits." Rose's voice trailed off as he searched Doc's face.

"KIA, shit, there's been so many, I can't remember when he bit it, but his fucking love beads weren't no match for an AK. Yeah, dead, in a really fucked-up operation not too far from where you got sapped."

"I've got some of the guys' addresses. Shit, after all this we gotta stay in touch," Rose said, quickly moving on as the memories and faces of men from his old unit began to flood his brain. The release he felt, being able to talk with someone he'd known before his hospitalization, had his emotions moving at full speed.

"How about Wagner? Now there was a really funny dude. Remember when he took that bet with Cowboy? Said he could ride that dink's water buffalo? Right outside Cam Lo, you remember that little villa...bad place, always took fire from that fucking spot. Should have napalmed the whole fucking rat hole, shit...don't know why we didn't round up every gook in the area, put them in the middle of the damn collection of mud huts and call in napalm! Remember"?

Doc's lips formed slowly. "Wagner and Cowboy's both dead. Cowboy got hit crossing a stream, fucking thing was flooded. Bad fight, we took a lot of casualties—by the time we got to him he'd either bled to death or drowned. Don't know which." He drew a long, slow breath. "Wagner sat on a 155. Gooks had it wired...and he was gone. Shit, we didn't even have to call a dust off. Wasn't nothin' to evacuate. Bits of this, pieces of that...largest part we found was a forearm and hand, and that was just luck. Not even his boots, I mean, we never found his feet. Fuckin' 155, that fucking round could take out a house or a whole block...but one guy. Shit."

"Sergeant Lifer, what the hell was his name?" Rose's voice was moving fast with excitement as the flood of news and information about former confederates became available.

"Dead, I hear." Doc's expression stayed flat. "Listen," Doc said, as if finally getting frustrated, "it's easier to say who's alive than dead. Cause most everyone's dead, or blown to shit like you, and anyway, I'm not ready to talk all this crap. You know what, Rose? Fucking Bravo Company, First Battalion Ninth Marines Regiment had twenty-two fucking men left in December! Twenty two! And of that number, most were so sick with gook rot of all sorts, they couldn't stand. You know, dysentery, round worm, malaria, and who knows what else? Shit, they all should have been hospitalized. So fucking sick. For all practical purposes the whole fucking company was wasted!"

Doc took a deep breath and continued to talk. "The fucking only assholes who got out of there alive were the ones who shoulda got sapped: Dipshit psychos like Gunther and his kiss-ass sidekick, fucking Bones Bradley. I guess Bones rotated back to the world... shit, about a month and a half or two before I got this," the Doc waved at the place where his calf was supposed to be attached to his knee, "and Gunther re-upped for another tour, shit, he couldn't get enough of Nam."

Rose felt tired. The excitement of running into an old friend was evaporating. The news was too depressing and he could tell that Doc was none too pleased to rattle off the numbers of the dead. They both needed some peace. "Hey, I gotta get some rest, and pretty soon they're serving chow, so, I'll see you at dinner mess and we'll talk about something positive...like getting laid." Rose tried to get a smile out of the Doc. Struggling with his walker, he finally positioned himself to face the aisle and lurched to his bed. As he turned and shuffled toward his bunk, the crushing weight of memory caused fatigue to rack his emaciated bones.

"Rose!" the voice bellowed. "Fucking Gunther was the one who did it. I didn't know. Honest. Just asshole Gunther and his group of chicken-shit jerk offs. There might have been a few who knew about it afterward, but it was those, um, those—" he stopped as he counted silently to himself "...seven pricks who were in on it. Gunther put them up to it, he was their God, but we didn't know 'til afterward."

"What are you talking about?" Rose stopped and partially turned to the crippled medicine man.

"Don't play stupid," Doc Wood growled, "you know damn

good and well what I'm talking about. I'm just sorry there wasn't anybody with the balls to call off the shit. But hell, like I said, only those suck-ass goofs that hung with Gunther knew for sure, and you know they weren't about to cross him. They thought he was God—or maybe the whole damn group were fags. Shit, I bet any one of them would have sucked Gunther's cock, all he had to do was ask. Real warriors, that group. But what I'm talking about is true: only those guys *knew*, but once you were gone they had to brag. You know, tough guys, with the implied threat that the same fate awaited anyone who crossed Gunther's path. Gunther was tough. No doubt. Shit, that was his second tour, and like I said, I guess he went in for a third. Couldn't keep him out of the bush. Some people are just that way. Nam fucked him up, he was real mental. All that power, point a finger, things disappear, shit, he was God with a capital 'G,' must have had a continual hard-on. I mean, who needs sex when you've got all that power? Those assholes around him were just hanging on, nothing special about them, but that fucker was tough and scary, that much is sure—Gunther...now there was a mean bastard. He was like a damn vampire, he just loved the blood, he couldn't get enough of it. Just wasn't meant to die, he loved the fight; shit, in the other world, the stateside world, he'd be strapped to a gurney and presented to medical students as a freak. Fuck, who needs Martians? Hope he gets sapped on this tour, I mean, some day this war's going to end, then what do you do with the Gunthers it created? He's better off staying in the bush permanently, or getting wasted. There's no place in the universe for him now—he's crossed over!"

Rose studied Wood carefully and then measured his words. "I don't disagree with you Doc, and I know Gunther didn't especially like me, but so what? I mean, what's your point? The war fucked up lots of guys...hell, who are we kidding, nobody's gonna spend thirteen months doing what we did and be normal...and hell, Gunther's been there for years. We're fucked for life, some mental, some physical, and guys like you and me get it from both ends. Shot to shit and psycho, both. But hell, I don't hold Gunther responsible for me. Shit, I hardly remember what happened that afternoon, but the gooks were there, and Gunther damn sure didn't send for them. It was an ambush, and I had the misfortune of being on point. So what?"

"You really don't know, do you? Well, life's a cluster fuck, Nam's the worst, and you got the fucking of your life. For a smart New York Jew, you're sure one dumb fuck. You mean you really *never* knew? And everyone was sure you were dead, I mean, I was there! Shit, I didn't give you a Chinaman's chance. They were all so sure you'd die, and hell, why not, you were as messed up as anyone I ever saw. Anyway, Gunther and his group were counting on it, especially after the lieutenant found out. Boy, he was pissed, but it don't much matter, I mean the lieutenant was wasted two or three weeks later, so he wasn't gonna talk. He got shot once, clean through and through, head hit. Boom down. No one saw it, they said it was a sniper, and I guess it could have been, but most of the company thought it was Gunther. But dead men don't talk, and shit, most guys we were with are dead, so you can't prove shit. Anyway, it's all months' old now, so you ain't got shit to work with except rumors, but I swear to Christ, it's true."

Rose waited, expecting the story to continue, but the Doc just ran his fingers through his hair and bowed his head.

"Boy oh Christ, you talk a lot, but you haven't said shit about this big secret, so how do I fit in this picture? So far all I know is that Gunther was a psycho, lots of good men are dead, and you and I are in this fucking hospital, I guess better off than most. So what's your point?"

"No pin!" Doc bellowed. "You stupid bastard, you didn't have a firing pin. Your rifle was fucked; they took out your pin! Maybe they put it back in, I don't know exactly what they messed up, but they screwed it up somehow...your 16 wouldn't fire...don't you see, they wanted you dead! I guess when you were sleeping somebody must have grabbed your weapon and screwed up the operating system...I don't know, but we both know the thing didn't work! Right? It's that simple. Why do you think you were stuck a hundred yards out on point? Did Gunther and his men come to your aid? Now you know, and I ain't saying any more, that's all I know, and that's enough. Jesus, what a fucked-up war. Don't ask me no questions, just know for sure I ain't bullshitting you, this happened, and if you think about it, you'll know it's true. Shit, are you dumb, and I guess that's the way Gunther planned it, but you were supposed to die. No witnesses. Just dead Marines. Gotta hand it to Gunther, he might have been smarter than all of us. And tougher. Jesus, even *I* wish you were dead, at least I wouldn't have to tell you this shit! But I'm done, now leave me alone for a while!"

Rose started to say the word, but "what" stuck in his throat. Three times he tried, only to get as far as "wha—." Doc Wood had his hands over his ears, signaling that he didn't want to hear another question. Mark Rose staggered to his bunk.

Like a bolt of lightning, within a slice of a second, many unanswered questions were put in place. At the speed of light, the fractured mosaic began to gel as his head whirled and the totality of events enveloped his skull. So simple. Yet, so complete. Like a jigsaw puzzle with lost pieces, newly discovered parts forced the picture to come into focus. His head pounded, as if being concussed with the power of a dozen chi-com grenades. Of course, he thought, distantly recalling rank comments by Marines: "you're dead, mother fucker," and "have a great time on point," "nice knowing you."

As if he were a part of a video car crash, where he could replay the event time and again, Rose pieced together the whole event. Bit by bit the circumstances that had ruined his life were forced upon him in a manner that made the term "disbelief" a living joke. Marines, led by the maniacal Gunther, had sent him to his death. The "whats" and "ifs" could never be answered, but now the certainty of that day was exposed for its simplistic terror.

What to do? Who to tell? Was it possible that Wood was wrong? Was there anyone left to confirm the event? Too many questions swirled in Rose's head. He fumbled with the top of the safety cap to his pain pills. His crippled hands shook and failed to dislodge the plastic cover as he swore under his breath. Finally, the vial opened. He studied the label for a moment: "Take one pill every six hours, as needed for pain." He reached for his water glass and downed four capsules before drifting off into a deep sleep.

Eighteen hours later, he awoke from a dreamless coma. He felt oddly refreshed as he turned and let his feet touch the tile floor. Somehow, the order of events from yesterday's discussion with the Doc was sublime and nearly docile. Shakily, he got to his feet and steadied himself on his walker. More information from Wood was necessary to fill in the blanks. He closed his blue hospital robe and shuffled down the corridor for a meeting with destiny.

He turned the corner into the room where he'd met Doc Wood the day before. Benches in the hallways held the twisted bodies of the "flower power" generation. The Tet Offensive raged, and the hospitals continued to fill and overflow. Where the Doc had been was a body in a full-length cast; only tubes came from the mass of gauze, and it struck Rose that he'd seen this picture before in a *National Geographic* magazine depicting Egyptian mummies.

"Where's Wood?" the little man asked a passing orderly.

"Who's Wood?" the hurried medical technician replied. "There's so fucking many bodies, I don't know names. Shit, guys come in and out of here faster than a New York subway train."

Rose could see that the medical man had little time for idle chat. It was obvious that he also was becoming a casualty of the Viet Nam war. You didn't have to serve "in country" to have your life totally altered. Six weeks of tending the wounded in the Balboa Navy Hospital could do plenty of damage.

"The medical guy," Rose said, "—name is Wood, had a bad leg...or I should say he didn't have a leg from the knee down. He was just here yesterday, maybe he's been moved."

The orderly flipped through pages on his clipboard, slowly

moving his finger past dozens of names, and finally came to a halt. "Wood, lost his leg with Ninth Marines, right?"

"Yeah, that's him," Rose replied. "Where is he?"

"Shipped to somewhere in the midwest, probably Kansas City—it's the only place with any room left. But, hell, who knows where he was sent, all his chart says is that, barring complications, he'll live, and they'll recommend 50 percent disability. Hell, I wonder how many arms and legs a guy has to lose to get 100 percent? Looks like he left about twelve hours ago."

"Can you find out where he is? It's important to me," Rose said, but knew instinctively that he'd muttered the wrong thing.

"Oh fuck yes," the orderly snapped, "I got plenty of time to look for the world's cripples! As you can see, I got nothing to do, lots of spare time—maybe I can just drop everything and go on a quest for missing persons. Hell, I read about these new computer things, supposed to be a magical machine, said some day we'd be able to find everyone with a push of the button! Imagine that? Listen Marine, all I know is, he's gone, and there's plenty more to take his place! And from the looks of you, you're going to have plenty of time to look up old war buddies...like a lifetime, cause you're fucked up for life! An invalid. Ward of the V. A. Shit, you do the looking, I got holes to plug."

MAY 1999

"Mr. Rose, Mr. Rose." Dr. Khali spoke with some urgency. "You seem to have drifted off. You must have been dreaming, but while you slept your records arrived. That's good and bad. I think it's best that we hold you for observation; as you know, your condition is serious and deteriorating.

Mark Rose woke up in the present, as the thirty-year-old Balboa nightmare faded. Slowly, he came to grips with his situation.

"Doc, I don't have time to be observed. I have an agenda, and it doesn't allow for my staying in your lovely new hospital. Now, if you can just get me my meds, I'll be on my way."

"It's not that easy, really. We want to give you the best treatment possible, and to do so we'll need your help. We can't just give you some pills because you say you know what's best for your condition, that wouldn't be very professional, and we wish to give you the best care we can. We owe you that; the V.A. really believes we owe a debt of gratitude to all you Viet Nam veterans. After all, the bleeding you've reported can only mean that something has gone wrong. With your list of injuries, the hemorrhaging could be from any number of sources." The swarthy-skinned doctor stopped and waited for the aging cripple to respond. Without so much as a word, the frail veteran pulled to his feet and moved off toward the exit.

The medical man stood, staring, as he grasped for words. Using impeccable Queen's English, Dr. Khali's voice became elevated and his words stern. "Mr. Rose, you have very serious problems and I suggest you reconsider, for time is crucial here."

"Yes, I know," the limping, former Marine said, "you didn't have to remind me of that. I appreciate the speech, but my time won't allow for the type of help you're recommending." Carrying the weight of terrible memories and a resolve to even the score, the little man wove his way through the corridors of aging veterans, back to his car, and drove down to the center of the city of Portland.

The air was warmer now—after all, it was nearly lunchtime. He'd spent over three hours at the V.A., and from that experience he'd only learned one thing: he would have to speed up his plans, for he had less time than he had originally thought. It would mean more risks, but what was the down side? How could he lose? After all, he was dying, and his only real enemy was time. He bought a sandwich and a coke and decided to sit outside the deli in the sun. He was not familiar with Portland; all he had was a map and some tourist information he'd gotten before he had left the east coast on his quest.

Students from Portland State University strolled past him as the sun warmed his weary bones. He needed to eat, needed the nourishment and strength. There was work to do, and the sharp pains that racked his guts reminded him of the ticking clock. As he sat, slowly chewing his food, he was touched by a melancholy feeling of serenity that was brought on by the youthful laughter and carefree frivolity of the passing students. It struck the dying man that he'd never had that experience—careless youth, young and in love—certainly his life had been no "Moveable Feast." By the time he was the age of most of these kids, all he'd known was the death of others, and by the time he was twenty, his own survival was in question as he languished in a Naval Hospital in Guam. If he didn't die there, he'd be moved to the hospital at San Diego. After his medical discharge from the Marines, he'd gone to school and earned his degree in business. After all, he was inclined towards accounting, it ran in his family. In fact, his uncle, a partner in a prestigious New York financial firm, had promised him a job. Hell, with his family connections, a young Mark Rose could have easily avoided any military duty. Gotten a phony deferment, or joined the reserves. Becoming a reservist during the Viet Nam years, was just a legal way of avoiding your duty to your country. But he went anyway, earning himself a degree of self-respect, but losing any help he could have gleaned from his well-to-do family. He was lectured over and over about the importance of being Jewish, and the lesson was reinforced by making it clear that Jews *didn't* join the military. The thought of him being drafted horrified everyone in his family. Being drafted into the Army was a gentile condition, and one that was not his concern. Let someone else do it. Mark Rose had other ideas, so at nineteen he had avoided the draft. He joined the Marines. The only member of his family to have been accepted into this elite body. That certainly made him proud, but it left his family in disbelief.

Three young girls sat at a table near his. In the half-dreamlike state of his mid-day drifting he listened in on their discussions. He could hear just enough words to know the college students were talking about boys they knew or wanted to know. Hushed whispering followed by shrieks of laughter let Rose know some sort of passionate secret was being passed from one young co-ed to the next. The wind changed, and he smelled the fragrance of female youth: a hint of perfume, body lotion, and cream rinse for the lustrous hair that glistened in the bright sun. He didn't stare. But he caught glimpses of their bright white teeth and the creamy skin that softly hinted at what marvelous pleasures must be hidden beneath the girls' clothing.

One of the girls nodded as she cupped her mouth and said something in her friend's ear. Within seconds, each student turned to look in his direction. They tried to be inconspicuous, even polite, but he'd seen it before. The girls pretended to look beyond him at some unseen item of interest. But Rose felt the eyes fall on him. The sun must have been just right to give maximum exposure to the faded purple scar that ran from the top of his head to his chin. It was ugly. He was ugly, and the huge facial gash was a visible example of what the rest of his body looked like. The girls turned away, and Rose quickly remembered how young kids would come up to him and just stare. Little ones, five years old. But they didn't know any better, it wasn't their fault...in his life it was only the inconsiderate adults that asked point blank, "What the fuck hit you?"

Rose glanced down at his wrist. Nearly one o'clock, with any luck he'd find his next quarry this very afternoon. The phone book's yellow pages gave him the address, and all he now needed was confirmation of employment and directions. The records from the last regimental reunion had listed the man's employer as Coliseum Ford. But that last gathering at Camp Pendleton was over three years ago, so the man may have moved or changed jobs.

Finishing his food, and passing by the table of girls for one last smell of youth, Rose limped to a nearby phone booth and dialed the number of the dealership. He felt the need to urinate, and he knew his shattered bladder was working overtime to process the combination of piss and blood.

"May I speak to Larry Keen?" Mark Rose politely asked the receptionist. There was a pause and a shuffling of paper.

"What was the name again, *Keen*? Which department does he work in, I'm kinda new here, and I'm not familiar with that name," the female voice droned.

"He should be in sales, a sales manager I think," Rose said, as he did a quick mental check of his facts.

"Let me transfer you to the sales office; I don't see that name on my list, so maybe someone up there can help." Without waiting for a reply, Rose was put on hold as the phone rang at the sales desk.

"Sales, can I help you?" a deep voice answered.

"I'm looking for Larry Keen, and the receptionist said you could help...he's an old friend."

"Keen hasn't worked here in about two years, but I know where he is, want the number?"

"Oh, yeah, that would be great; he's still in town then?" Rose jotted down the number of the Ford dealership that Keen was supposed to be working at, and asked if the place was nearby. He jotted down directions and thanked the man.

Mark Rose went to a Texaco station and asked to use the bathroom. His bladder pulsed. The young black female clerk was talking on the phone, obviously to a friend, as she asked the scarred customer what he needed.

"I already told you," his irritation boiling over, "I need to use the bathroom, and if you weren't so busy goofing off on the phone you would have heard me."

Sensing a chance to get even with the rude client, the girl replied, "Restrooms are for customers only sir; are you getting gas?"

"No, I'm not getting fucking gas! But I need to piss—now do your goddamn job and let me in the head!"

"You ain't no customer, and you can't talk to me like that, now you get your ugly, road-map face out of here, or I'm calling the cops. Now git!"

Rose swung toward the door, his insides pounding, his head a mass of visceral confusion. As he passed the candy rack he pulled as hard as he could, sending the display to the floor. "Fuck you, nigger!" he yelled, "and don't think I won't be back. You fucked with the wrong guy!" He couldn't have noticed that the strain of the destructive effort had caused his swollen bladder to let loose a stream of urine and blood that followed him as he trudged to his waiting car. As he drove away he could see the frantic clerk pointing at his car as she screamed into the phone. He thought to himself how stupid his actions were. Shit, if he were to have a chance at finishing his "job," he'd have to be discreet, not make a fool of himself at a service station. Now the attendant had probably called the cops. All he could hope for was that she didn't get his license plate number, and that the local cops were too busy to concern themselves with a crippled name caller. *How dumb can you be?* Rose asked himself. And to suggest an implied threat of his return—what was he thinking? It wasn't until he was on the freeway headed west, and a few minutes away from the Texaco station, that he saw the damp reddish-colored stains on his pants or felt the pain that throbbed through his entire mid-section.

"Larry Keen, please." The phone rang, and the voice said she'd see if Keen was in yet. She wasn't sure of his schedule, but at least Rose knew where the Beaverton-area car dealer was and the reunion was near at hand. As he waited for what seemed an eternity, he tried to envision how Keen might look today. A blond skinny kid, that's all he really remembered. Quick to laugh, and long legs, kept up a good hump. *Now,* he thought to himself, *I'm waiting to kill him.*

Somehow, all Rose's victims were frozen in time, and at night, as he lay awake, he only pictured them as nineteen-year-old kids, yet filthy grunts...and good killers. They were all conspirators, the ones who had helped Gunther—of that he was sure. And now, with nothing to lose, he was here to even the score. The picture was clear, and the mission well defined. The race was with time.

"This is Larry Keen, can I help you?" The voice was not recognizable. *Why would it be?* Rose wondered. It had been over thirty years, and he never really knew any of these men when he'd served with them in Viet Nam. After all, he'd only been in Viet Nam for about two months before being wounded. Suddenly, it occurred to Rose that there could easily be more than one Larry Keen, and he temporarily froze. He'd have to be careful, no mistakes—he'd know Keen's face once he spotted him.

After a moment's hesitation, Rose stumbled as he haltingly said, "I need a car."

"Well, I'll refer you to a salesman, and we'll go from there," the frustrated voice replied. "I mean, I'm a desk manager, so it's best you talk to one of our salespeople; they'll help you."

"No, I was referred to you, so I'd like to come in and talk about a purchase." Rose knew he'd have to act fast; he hadn't expected the direction of the discussion, and knew he was getting nowhere and sounding stupid.

"Really" Keen said, "who referred you? I always like to send a little something special to those folks."

"I'll tell you when I get there," Rose replied. "It's an old friend and I want to make it a real surprise. So how late do you work?"

"OK, surprise me, I'm here 'til at least nine, probably later, so come in and give me a thrill," Larry Keen answered, as the little cripple on the other end of the line sighed in relief. Darkness would be on his side.

Mark Rose spent several hours looking over the area near the auto dealership. The business itself was too well lit to offer any type of opportunity for what Rose needed to accomplish. Another plan would need to be hatched. About six blocks from the car lot was a sloppy-looking bar that appeared to have little or no lighting in the parking area. Rose went in the side entrance and allowed his eyes to become focused in the darkened room. There were few people at the counter; the bartender eyed him closely.

"Gimme a Bud," Rose said before the man could ask, "a small one."

There was nothing remarkable about the bar. Just a neighborhood tavern with the usual video poker machines, poster pin-up girls, cheap wine, and the stinking smell of stale cigarettes.

The bartender delivered the glass. "That'll be a buck fifty, or you can start a tab," the man said as he smiled narrowly.

"Thanks, I think I will tab it for a few minutes, wait for the traffic to die down. What time is it, anyway?"

"Quarter to seven," the bartender replied, "but this is Beaverton, and traffic is so fucked up you may have to stay until closing before it starts to taper off. Ain't seen you before. Must not be from around here." The man waited for a reply.

"No, I'm just passing through, on my way to Seattle to visit some real old friends. Kind of a "Sentimental Journey"—guys I haven't seen in years." Rose couldn't help but notice the man looking at his disfigured face. The years had allowed the scars to fade, but even in the dim-lit bar the criss-crossed purple gashes were obvious. The bartender didn't ask, and for that Rose was thankful.

"Where's the bathroom?" Rose asked. "Bladder's full already."

"You walked right past it on the way in, just around the corner. You want another Bud?"

"Yeah, but this time make it a pint. Didn't think it would taste this good."

When he returned, the bartender was bantering with several men part way down the counter. The guys were young, under thirty, and on closer inspection they had that predictable look about them that screamed "car salesman." Rose listened in as the group recalled some stupid event that they found amusing. The sun was moving lower in the sky when other men arrived. More car salesmen. Obviously, all the people knew each other, and as they swapped different car stories, Rose finished his second beer. Had to piss again. Not much bladder left.

An hour passed. By now it was evident that the bar was a favorite watering hole for salespeople from the nearby Ford dealer. Rose recognized there was an opportunity here but that it was fraught with danger. He could ask if anyone knew Keen, but the risk would be enormous. He could blow his cover, but on the other hand, he could find out that the Larry Keen he'd planned to kill that night was the wrong guy. After all, the information he'd retrieved from Marine Corps archives at Camp Pendleton was years old. Two of his intended victims were nowhere near their last reported address. He'd not had the time or energy to track them down further, he had limited opportunity, so he'd had to move on to other targets. With the knowledge he'd gleaned from the Marine personnel office, there were several others to "visit." Mostly, he'd wanted Gunther. But Keen also was high on his list. His bladder ached. The bartender again approached.

"Another?" he asked in a friendly tone.

"OK, one more, then I should go. Looks like your business is filling up with car people," Rose commented offhand.

"Yeah, you got that right. Shit, if it weren't for that car place we'd be out of business in a week. Never seen so many addicts, must be a hell of a job. The bosses are the worst. Middle-age ass-holes, most of them, burned out druggies that take special plea-sure in insulting people and thinking they know everything in the world. Some are OK, but most of these guys are jerks, losers, or they'd have got out of that business years ago. But, shit, who am I to talk, here I am forty years old, pumping beer."

One of the growing number of drunks seemed to have the floor. Loud and boisterous, he kept telling inane stories that spoke to his limited lease on life. *This man is stupid*, Rose thought. The only thing more repulsive was the childlike audience. Grown men laugh-ing at the most pedestrian of suggestions confirmed for Rose his pre-conceived notion of the auto industry. Filled up with a special type of personality that defied most analysis.

Darkness was nearly complete and Rose had a choice to make. He'd thought over his options carefully, and decided it would make no sense to mention Keen's name. He was close to his prey; a little patience and he'd know if his man was at hand. Just then another group of men entered the tavern.

"Well, looky here," one patron exclaimed as he swiveled on his bar stool, "if it ain't deskman extraordinaire Larry Keen! Shit, there goes the neighborhood."

The men passed by Rose and exchanged short, cutting insults about each others' wives, selling ability, and waistlines. Good-hearted pats on the back were delivered, and another round of beer soon followed. The short cripple studied the group closely, trying to figure out who the man named Keen was in the crowd. The room was dark and filling with smoke...no one took any notice of him as he looked for a sign of recognition that had been buried for three decades. His hands trembled with excitement as his brain went into warp speed, and his life passed by his face. *Like a traffic accident*, he thought to himself; *it happens so fast, you're just part of the picture, but your life seems to pass before you in that moment.* In rapid, machine-gun-like bursts that flooded his memory, filled his eyes, and seared his brain, he went into another time and place.

His father and mother. An uncle, and an arm around his shoulder. Smiles and laughter as they walked through the accounting office, his uncle pointing to a desk that would someday be his for the asking. Screaming voices in the family home as he announced his enlistment in the Marine Corps. The importance of being Jewish. His family emphasizing his privileged position, not many Jews served in the military, you could make money...lots of money, if he'd just stay with his family, learn the business. Military service was beneath him, it was for other, less capable people. In the worst case situation, his father could get him in a reserve outfit. The reserves were the elites' way of legally dodging the draft. Terror, as smoke and explosion closed in on him outside the hill of Cam Lo. Recovery, two years of therapy, Doc Wood, firing pins, a successful academic period, followed by a lucrative job from a forgiving family, and marriage to Debbie.

Debbie, why had he become involved with her? He knew from the beginning that she was there for his earning potential, certainly not love. Just money. Years passed, his condition deteriorated, and loving Debbie made it clear that she would rejoice in his death. A screaming wife, increasingly contemptuous of him, calling him deformed, mocking his inability to sire children, constantly telling him he should have had his whole dick blown off, adultery, open affairs, and in the final stages of their marriage, pictures to prove her infidelity. Diagnoses from Veterans Hospitals, failing kidneys, more operations, the good and the bad news about the time he could expect to live. Debbie filing for divorce, getting most of his hard-earned assets, termination from his job, all the heartfelt apologies, but surely he'd understand...he was missing so much work, the company couldn't afford to carry him further. Too much hospital time, too much convalescing, and a prediction of more health problems to come. Income going from eighty thousand a year to 100-percent service-related disability. Postcards from Debbie and her new boyfriend from the Mediterranean, saying "Wish you were here...sucker." One final task. So far, four dead bodies. Four old scores that needed to be settled. Four ears tucked in plastic. Two more former comrades to dispose of, and a fading period of time to accomplish the payback.

"Want another, buddy?" The bartender snapped him from his tortuous daydream.

"Yeah, sure, I guess one more can't hurt at this point." Rose cleared his head and focused on the business at hand. He peered into the crowd of car salesmen, determined to see if the Keen he sought was among the group. Enough banter and chatter was being exchanged for him to isolate Keen, whose back was turned toward him. He knew from experience not to see them as they were thirty years ago and to have no preconceived notion of what they'd appear like now.

His beer came and he thanked the bartender. Rose turned to the counter and took a long drink of the cold brew. As he swiveled toward the loud group of men, Keen moved his head and presented a profile. The nose. He saw its shape first. The bridge was nearly concave, they used to tease him, call him banana nose and ski jump. Staring hard, he looked for other clues. The banana-nosed guy moved, and in an instant Rose knew he'd found the man who had haunted his dreams.

Slow down, he thought to himself. *Nurse the beer, no time to get drunk, I need a clear head.* He went to the bathroom, took a leak, and splashed cold water on his face. Staring into the mirror, Rose looked hard at his dripping reflection then glanced sideways in search of a towel. No paper towels were attached to the walls, just a blow-dry machine; Rose cursed under his breath. Just then the door opened and another patron entered the men's room. Larry Keen.

Rose froze. His mind traveled. Water ran off his chin. Keen passed within a foot of the cripple on his way to the urinal.

"No fucking towels," Rose mumbled, just loud enough for the balding blond man to hear. "No towels to dry with, I suppose that's why bar napkins were invented." Rose wiped the water from his face on the sleeve of his shirt. He loosened up, for the fear of recognition was impossible, it had been thirty years and all of his old unit assumed that he was dead. The opportunity to engage Larry Keen presented itself, as Keen responded to the little man at the mirror.

"Yeah, well none of the guys here are gonna notice much how you look, I mean you could be totally soaked and these drunks wouldn't have a clue." Keen spoke for the first time. As he talked, he turned his head and looked at Rose.

The scarred man looked back at Keen, who was stepping from the stall. It was obvious that Keen was not looking at Rose's damp face, but seeing past that to the disfigured head that more resembled a road atlas than human form. Nothing unusual there, he'd endured that for over thirty years. The man in front of him was partly responsible for Rose's pain...and now it was time to pay. Rose scanned the face for any signs of recognition. There were none. He was safe, but he'd have to change all his plans. His mind went into overdrive. When the body would be found, questions would be asked. He was now a known figure at the bar, how hard would it be to recall a little guy with a face like his? Police would reconstruct the evening, and certainly the bartender and others would remember a scarred-up limping stranger that they'd never seen before or since. If they stumbled upon the V.A., his visit there would certainly start the search, and maybe the puzzle would begin to take form. Really, he was somewhat amused that some-body hadn't figured him out by now. He'd read of a detective in San Diego who was assigned to the case in Southern California, but the last he'd heard was the dead, one-eared veteran's case was wide open. He had a total of four ears in his car, he needed two more. Then he thought, *so what if I get caught? What will they do?* He had maybe two or three months to live... The problem was not getting caught, but rather delaying his apprehension long enough to finish this one final mission. He had two more men to settle this score with, and one of them was standing before his eyes.

There was nothing to do but go back to the bar. He needed time to sort out a quick change in plans. The beer was cold, however none of it mattered now, all he could think of was how to calm his anxiety, to step back and think. Music played in the background but Rose didn't hear it, laughter and shouts punctuated the night but all he could focus on was a nervous ache and an information overload that slit his head.

Slow down. Nobody has any idea who you are, or why you're here. After several minutes his heart began to slow, and his breathing returned to near normal. His only goal now became to get out of the bar quickly, but without causing a scene. *Think. No mistakes, act casual.* He finished his beer, swiveled on the stool, and walked quickly out the side door into the night. His leg dragged behind him, but he made it to the car and fumbled for his keys.

"Hey, where you goin' cowboy?" a voice bellowed. Rose turned just as he unlocked the door. The bartender stood in front of him with an angry look on his face.

"What do you mean?" Rose answered, "I've had enough, gotta go home."

"Well, buddy, that's fuckin' great, but how about paying your bill? That drink-and-dash shit don't go over big here." Behind the angry man, shapes of other people could be seen standing in the doorway. Several of the men moved to the bartender's side, one of them being Keen. There would be no physical problem from the cripple; the bartender hardly needed any help.

"I'm sorry, shit, I just forgot," Rose stammered, "really, I've got the money, I've got too much on my mind. Shit, I'm sorry." He dug in his pocket, hands shaking, and cursing under his breath. *What an idiot, now the whole world's staring at you, and you didn't want to attract attention. Shit, this is one for the books.*

A twenty-dollar bill was stuffed into the man's hand. "Keep the change," Rose said, "and I'm really sorry, shit, I've got too much going on. I'm sorry." The glaring bartender turned and walked toward the bar, muttering "asshole" for all to hear.

Rose slid into the seat of his car. Panting and sweating, he waited for his system to slow down, trying to collect his thoughts. All he could think of was to flee the area, and by the time he began to gain some focus, he was miles away from the tavern, not knowing where he was, or where he was going.

Rose was awoken by the strains of his bladder. He rolled and looked at the bedside clock. Two thirty. The neon flickering of the motel sign oriented him to the small room. Staggering to the bathroom, he loosened a stream of blood and urine into the toilet. Shaky, he grabbed for his remaining medications and swallowed what was left. *Not much time.*

He returned to the bed and sat on its edge. A new plan was necessary, but for that he knew that he would need sleep. There were two more jobs left to do, and his abilities were fading with each day. His condition was terminal. Without the medications the process would speed up, and the collective injuries sustained thirty years before would take him from the planet. He drew on whatever inner strength he could, finally focusing on the pivotal point of his life. *You're a Marine,* he said to himself, *nothing is impossible for a Marine. There are no ex-Marines, only former Marines; be tough...two more missions for you, Marine.*

It was nine o'clock when he again opened his eyes. Six Excedrin and the last of his meds had allowed a deep sleep. His mid-section throbbed. His bones ached, and the unsteady rise to his feet reminded him of how vulnerable he'd become. Still, he was a Marine, and he had a job to do.

Rose spent the afternoon relaxing. Sitting on park benches and enjoying the warm spring air. He tried to think of a workable plan for Keen's execution, but knew there was not going to be an easy answer. This would have to be trial and error. He'd wait until well after dark to position himself for a clear view of the tavern's lighted parking lot. There was no guarantee that Keen would again go to the pub, but from what he'd seen the night before, there seemed a pretty good chance that the car salesmen's activities were predictable.

Rose would stay sober, he would not be seen, and when the time was right, he would end Larry Keen's life. An image of Gunther's face crossed his memory. Gunther was supposed to live right across the river in Vancouver—he was close, just a few lucky breaks and his job would be over.

Like clockwork, at nine thirty, four men arrived in the tavern parking lot. Rose could clearly pick out Keen, still marveling at how much weight he'd gained. But then, thirty years changes just about everything, and Rose felt no need to become nostalgic. He felt the bull-barreled Ruger .22 between his seats. The weapon had performed perfectly, an assassin's dream, really, so easy to silence, and hard to trace. A factory-adapted brass catcher insured no shell casings were left at the scene, and reading between the lines of various newspaper accounts of his "work," he knew the police were baffled by this lack of evidence.

Hours passed, and this made Rose more confident. He knew time would result in his intended victim being more intoxicated. The chill that had come as the sun set and the night cooled made Rose crisply alert, and the coffee can he carried in the car prevented him from having to leave the vehicle to urinate. Rose knew he'd have to follow Keen; there wouldn't be a chance to do his job in the bright parking lot. How this was to happen, he wasn't sure.

After all, he had no idea where Keen lived or anything about his habits. All he knew was that time was short and his options were fading.

After midnight, Larry Keen left the bar. He walked unsteadily to his vehicle, and seemed to hesitate before he dropped into the seat. Rose followed his car and mused about how easy it must be for a cop to bust a drunk this time of night. Rose stayed several car lengths behind, and saw how deliberate and slow Keen was driving. *Too cautious*, he thought, as they weaved down streets, turning into an area of new housing and construction. *Even I can tell he's drunk, what an idiot.* The weaving car rolled down the street, pausing too long at intersections, making Rose wonder if the driver was lost. Keen turned into a driveway that bordered the last completed new house and the half-built subdivision that trailed up the avenue. Rose turned off his lights and rolled to a stop. There was no time to survey much of the area, he was committed, and unless a neighbor with insomnia was out strolling, he would do his job.

It was quiet and dark as Rose stuck the Ruger in his pants and walked as quickly as he could manage toward the parked car. He looked over his shoulder, turned and saw nothing as he moved into the driveway. Luck was with him; as he approached the driver's door he could hear Keen cursing the keys as he struggled to get out of the car. Rose waited, pulled out the gun, and caught Larry Keen as he exited the sedan.

"I've got a gun, shut the fucking door and move over toward the side of the garage," Rose commanded, as he glared into the face of a stunned Larry Keen. The driver hesitated as the shock of the moment sobered him at the speed of light.

"Who are you, I ain't got no money! What the hell's going on, this must be a mistake." Fear flowed from the man's mouth, as his eyes squinted in the dark.

"No mistake, asshole, now move or die." Rose subliminally thought how easy this process had become, and how confident he was of the outcome. The fearlessness of his voice surprised him for a moment, as he focused on the terror that was expressed in Keen's face.

"What do you want, do I owe you money?" Grasping for straws, Keen moved backward looking hard into the face of death. "In the bar, now I remember you, but shit I didn't chase after any money, that was the bartender, shit this is a mistake! I was just *there*, that's all, hell I don't give a shit if you never pay your bar tab! Please, you've got the wrong guy...Mike's his name, the bartender, he did it. I didn't do shit!"

"Shut up, it'll take a second to refresh your memory." Rose walked the frightened man around to the dark side of his garage. "We don't have long, Corporal Keen."

"What the fuck is going on here? Shit, I sell cars, I ain't a corporal of nothing, this is fucked up. You got me confused!" Keen half-smiled, a nervous grin that belied his terror. Maybe he thought it would make the little cripple think. A dog barked in the distance.

"Look at me," Rose snapped, "look at me real hard, Corporal, what do you see?" The gun was pointed directly at Keen's chest.

"Nothing, I don't see nothing, this is fucked, please...shit, I don't understand, all this over a beer tab!"

"No, it's a little more than that, Marine...it's payback for a long-overdue debt. There's not much time, now think!"

Rose could tell that the overcome man in front of him was too confused and scared to put together the picture, and he didn't have all night to prolong the agony. He'd get it over with, but not before letting Larry Keen know why he had to die. "Cam Lo." Rose paused for a second, long enough to see the flicker of recognition in the man's eyes. If you knew what it was, it would be a name that you'd never forget, and if you'd never heard it, Cam Lo would make no sense. He had his man.

"You left me, Corporal. You left L/Cpl Rose to die. I didn't die, obviously, but my life has been fucked by you and the likes of your buddy, Gunther, and it's time to reintroduce myself and time for you to say goodbye." Rose could see the time warp crossing Keen's face, as he traveled back to that hot July 1967 afternoon. Disbelief. Shock. A gaping jaw.

"I still don't get it." It was clear to Rose that the picture he wanted to paint for Larry Keen would take too much time, so the cripple had to help while enjoying the finality of the situation.

"I'm Rose, and you left me to die. Took my firing pin...ruined my life! Now do you get the picture, scumbag? I ain't got all night, but I want you to know some people have long memories and long arms. Think for a second, you've had a good life. I haven't. Really, you killed me years ago, it's just that my death took decades, and I've got just a few things left to do before I go. Now...do you remember?"

"Yeah, but it was Gunther," the terror spewing like saved-up vomit, "he did it, we just went along! Shit, this ain't real, you're dead. You're a ghost, what's going on here? Oh shit!" He was raising his voice.

"Shut up asshole." He could wait no longer. The slide to the Ruger slipped back and Rose pulled the trigger. The silenced .22 made no more noise than a pencil tapping on a wooden table. Two shots to the chest; Keen fell back against the garage and crumpled to the ground. *Small caliber rounds*, Rose thought, *the choice of the professional assassin, but I need to be sure.* He held the barrel five inches from the back of Keen's head. *Two more bullets. No time to waste.* Then he pulled the knife from his pocket, and sliced the dead man's ear clean.

Rose turned and moved quickly toward his car. *Clean*, he thought, as the quiet of the partially developed new construction closed in the night. At once he was struck by the urge to urinate. He had no choice, his nearly defunct bladder would not wait. In the darkness he unzipped his fly and peed a combination of blood and water on the ground and sidewalk. He turned the key of his car, and drove toward a motel, making mental plans for his last mission.

JUNE 1999

Dick Hand was looking forward to seeing his uncle. Uncle Bill
lived in Balboa, less than an hour north of San Diego, and his
nephew liked him a great deal. Hand was frustrated that he'd not
seen Uncle Bill in nearly four months. There was no excuse. Of
course he'd been busy; heavier case loads, fewer people, officers
retiring, and nagging unsolved murders hadn't given Hand time
to travel the short distance up the beautiful Southern California
coast. Uncle Bill would give him hell, he was sure of that. But
once the berating had concluded, they'd catch up on their mutual
activities.

Hand's uncle had never married. Bill was fifty-one years old,
and Hand's mother's brother. Girlfriends, yes. But no one was ever
able to get too close to him...a private man. He lived a simple life,
keeping a one-bedroom condo with a pull-out sofa for guests to stay
the night. If that wasn't good enough, then you could hit the road.
The lush colors of the California shoreline made Hand think of all
the reasons he loved living in this paradise. As he turned into his
uncle's driveway he saw Bill sitting on the small balcony, holding a
Budweiser.

"Well, no shit, little nephew," his laughing uncle bellowed, "glad you could get away from your duties! What the hell...you get promoted to chief or something? Too busy for old Uncle Bill?!"

They embraced, as his uncle produced a bottle of beer from out of nowhere.

Bill had been Hand's greatest supporter when he announced that he'd joined the police department. With each promotion, Uncle Bill would send heartfelt congratulations to his nephew and encourage him to perform with military precision. After attaining the rank of detective at such an early age, it was clear that Hand had found his calling and a stellar career was in the future. Uncle Bill's only regret for his favorite nephew was that he'd never served in the military. But in quiet, introspective moments, his uncle knew that the real reason for seeing his nephew in the service was so that he might share in a glimpse of his own experiences. Reality dictated that that would never happen, even if Dick Hand spent a lifetime in the service of this country. Still, with a career in law enforcement, Hand would know some of the emotion that was a huge part of his uncle's existence.

Three beers were consumed in a matter of minutes. Rough edges were removed and easy discussion of events in each man's life began to flow. Not much new with Uncle Bill. After retiring from the army, Bill settled into a low-key, comfortable lifestyle and augmented his income by writing for several magazines and doing guest columns for various veterans' publications. He was a highly decorated veteran of the Viet Nam war, and his name was well known in military circles. He never talked in detail about his combat experiences and had made it clear that no amount of prompting would change his position. The older Hand got, the more he respected his uncle's privacy, for he knew that Bill carried ghosts that were not meant to be shared with the uninitiated. The closest Dick Hand ever got to his uncle's traumas was through his writing and what those brief openings were revealing. Still, his experience on the police force gave him some idea of what his uncle must have gone through. That was enough.

After an hour or so, Hand began to talk about the case that was causing him nightmares. Not a single lead had turned up one clue, and the young detective knew his reputation was sliding each week. There had been oblique comments about removing him from the murder investigation and replacing him with "a more experienced man." Of course, that hadn't been done, for nobody familiar with the case wanted any part of the seemingly hopeless situation.

"I don't know," Hand offered after a fifteen-minute explanation of the Danny Miller fiasco, "there just doesn't seem to be anywhere else to go. I know the answer's in there somewhere, but I swear to Christ, I can't seem to turn up a damn thing." His uncle sat quietly and seemed to be pondering some far-off thought. He stood and walked to the open sliding glass door that looked upon the Pacific Ocean. The expression on his face made Dick Hand apprehensive. There appeared a distant, icy mosaic that rippled across his entire body.

"Sorry if I'm boring you," Hand said, and quickly moved toward the door. "Shit, I don't want to make this everyone's problem. My wife's going nuts, and I suppose it's something I'll have to live with. Just part of the job, but it's sure been tearing my ass up."

"How old did you say this dead guy was?" Bill asked.

"Just turned fifty, I think, or maybe late forties, something like that. Family man, had affairs on his wife..."

His uncle raised his hand, palm out, like a traffic cop. "Military?"

"Yeah, stinking decorated Marine, all the honors, and that's just one of the things that makes this so damn odd. Guy wasn't the type to have a hit man waste his ass. Viet Nam, hell around the same time you were there, not sure of the dates, but it's something close to that."

"What did he do in the Corps?" His uncle turned to him, resting his lower back on the railing.

"What do you mean? I don't have all the information, you

know, it was around thirty years ago. But he did a good job, like I said, decorated, has a silver star and two purple hearts, so *shit*, he was a good Marine, but so what? Like I said, that was a long time ago, and we're talking about a guy who was killed a few months ago."

Hand's uncle motioned his nephew toward the round table that was positioned at the end of the balcony. "Sit down," he said in a voice that left Dick little room for reaction. "You need another beer."

Bill returned with four beers, set them down, and pulled out a chair directly opposite his nephew. For a long protracted moment, Bill looked at Hand and, grabbing a beer, sighed and tilted back and rocked on the chair's hind legs. "Tell me about the Marine," he said, matter-of-factly.

"Like I said, good record, honorable discharge, lots of decorations, no PTSD that's on record, did three years, and got out. That's about it. He was a corporal when he was discharged, had a couple of minor infractions, but overall was a good jarhead. So, there's nothing really there to go on, and shit, it's a long time ago. Somebody wanted him dead *now*. Here, in 1999. What he did as a kid in the Corps must have been something, I mean, you were in Viet Nam, so you must know. Combat grunt, had to be tough, but that's not why he was killed, shit, that should make him a hero...and listen, Uncle Bill, I sound like a broken record, but that was a long time ago, and the story goes nowhere. Believe me, I've tried."

Stony silence and an icy expression greeted Hand. His uncle waited, and as Dick began to continue his description of Danny Miller, his uncle crossed his hands as if to motion for a time-out. A full minute passed.

"Have there been any other murders that even come close to this one?" Bill asked, looking past Hand into the distance.

"I don't want to sound like a know-it-all, Bill, but I've been doing this crap for quite a while. I know I'm young by your standards, but I know what I'm doing. No shit. I've seen all kinds of killings, and I won't bore you with details, but if you think for a minute I haven't compared this one with everything that's gone on before or since in this whole fucking area, you're nuts. And yes, I'm pissed. It's my job, Bill, of course I've checked everywhere, and come up with nothing! It's goddamn frustrating. Then people like you have to ask me stupid questions like...gee, have I checked other homicides? That's my job, there's nothing close to this stinking mystery in all southern California, there's just no reason that this guy had to die the way he did! None! Fuck! None of it makes sense, and there are no more fucking leads! Hell, I'm the detective, you think I haven't cross referenced this with everything from jaywalking to Area 51 space aliens? It's madness!"

Dick Hand was panting as he realized he'd been yelling at his remarkably composed uncle. Bill sat across from him and rubbed his chin as he took a large pull from his Budweiser. The wind chimes that Bill adorned his house with began to sing as the Pacific breeze blew over the two of them.

"You're wrong about one thing," Bill said slowly, "and I'm not pretending to know how to be a cop, but something's missing." He put down his empty bottle, and uncapped another beer. "This murder did not happen randomly, you're sure of that," he continued. "It was planned, you're the expert, and that's your conclusion, so there has to be a reason. Maybe there are no more leads, but something's missing with the ones you've got. I've got an idea, and if you've already checked it out, then I'll shut up, but for now, just listen."

Hand began to speak, but the change occurring on his uncle's face made him stop without uttering a sound. It was as if a different man was emerging from some unknown depth, a genie from a bottle was appearing and another form was twisting into existence. Hand did not dare to try and stop it, for a monster was taking shape, and it sent fear and shivers through his entire body.

"Let me tell you about ears," his uncle began, as his voice changed and a near metamorphosis began to consume the person who was here and now as he slipped into the nether world of another era.

"Terrible things were done in that place. Viet Nam. We were young, hell I was eighteen when I got in country. Eighteen. By the time I left the land I was twenty one, but even then I knew that I'd never leave. Really. Physically we left, but you can never really come home, Dicky boy. Let me tell you about ears." With that he stood up. "You gotta pee?" he asked. Hand shook his head. "Don't move, I'll be right back."

A few minutes passed, and his uncle returned to the table. He had a beer in hand and carried a small box tucked under his arm. "My box of medals," he said without making eye contact. "War does strange things to a man. I remember being sucked into another world, just like a brick had been thrown through a delicate glass window. Smash. The world I had known for eighteen years shattered, and like Humpty Dumpty, it never came back. No way to really explain, just a journey to places you never knew existed, doing things that you can't easily share, but it doesn't matter. No amount of rationalizing or explaining will ever bring anybody who wasn't there into that world. Can't be done. The old world blew apart, and somehow, those of us who went through that trip have carried on the best we can. But we're different, we can never come home, and in an odd way, most vets would admit they don't want to come back anyway. Life after Nam is one big bore. I really can't explain—there's no way anyone who didn't go would ever come close to the space I sit in. Sounds simplistic, I know, but that's it, really. You'll never know, and no amount of effort will ever bring you to my world. Viet Nam is part of my blood, my flesh. I eat it every day. So do lots of guys I know. Don't feel sorry for us, it's just that you'll never know us. We have a fraternal order that lies just beneath the surface of this world, and nobody who didn't walk the bush and stare at those terrifying mountains can ever join our group. No amount of books, no movies, no lectures, no nothing... just Nam."

A long pull on the bottle gave Dick the chance to say what he was thinking. "I don't doubt a word you're saying, but my concern is here and now, and out of due respect, shit, I know I'll never understand what you went through, but my guy, Danny Miller, wasn't killed for being a good Marine. It just doesn't make sense."

"You just don't get it, do you?" his uncle hissed.

"I guess not," Dick answered. "But I'm all ears, I'm listening. Tell me where this is going."

"All ears," his uncle grinned, "that's cute, I love that one. All ears."

Uncle Bill lovingly set the little box on the table. It was worn, not from handling, but was just an old box that looked like it could have once held cigars. Bill turned it gently, and softly muttered, "It's been a while."

The lid of the container was opened, but the flap faced Dick, so the contents were obscured. His uncle pulled what was clearly a picture from the box. A snapshot. He held it close to his face and smiled. After a moment he passed it to Hand. Not a word was spoken.

The grainy photo was of three men, all military, and all in very rough shape. The faces had blank stares, and the equipment they carried made it obvious that the picture was of soldiers in Viet Nam.

"In the middle," his uncle said, "that's me in the middle. One hundred forty pounds of dysentery-infected killing machine. Been in country over a year. Had every type gook disease known to man. God I was sick. Didn't need gooks to kill you, after a year of humping that bush the land itself killed you. The land was in cahoots with the sky, and the rain, and the jungle, the sun, leeches, snakes, unknown flying fucking bugs, God knows what else...no sleep, shit, it all ganged up on you. Hell, the country itself killed you. All the elements jumped you and wore you down, the dirt, the daily smell of death. It all joined to kill you. Then there were the gooks."

"Take a look at this." A second picture was passed and again it

showed men in tattered clothes, but this time they were pointing
to a pile of twisted dead Vietnamese. The soldiers were smiling,
but from the old worn photo, it was hard to see if the grins were
genuine, or if they were just sad expressions of resignation. The
lines were dark, and the men in the picture took on a surreal per-
sona that seemed from another planet.

A third photo was produced from the evil little box. Hand's
uncle passed it across the table. It showed him with a string of non-
descript items held in front of his chest. They seemed to be held
together by a strand of wire or some such material. Dick stared
for some moments, then looked up at his uncle. The picture was
of poor quality, and as Hand raised his head, his uncle began to
speak.

"Ears," he said. "They're ears of dead gooks. We had strings of
them. "Hung them all over our hooches as souvenirs: ears, tongues,
toes, body parts. Hell, we kept one dead dink in the corner, used
him for parts. The joke was 'assemble your own gook,' kinda like
Funny Mr. Potato Head. You're too young to remember, 'Put in an
eye, put in a nose, put in a mouth and away he goes...Funny Mr.
Potato Head.'" He paused, as if to let his nephew catch up.

"I know the tune," Dick replied, "Mr. Potato Head still had a
following when I was a kid...hell, I guess he still does, I see the T.V.
ads once in a while. But I never thought of the connection between
the kids' tubers and building your own human from body parts.
It's sick, and, first, I don't see why you're so proud of it, or what
the hell this has to do with anything today! I think we're getting
off track."

"Proud?" his uncle stiffened. "Proud isn't the word. You'll never
know, so there's no sense trying to take you places that you can't
go. The stretch is too great. But proud is just one of the words.
Yes, I guess we were proud, but to be proud of something like that,
you had to feel the heat...and all I've said to you has no meaning.
You just don't get it. You're a smart detective, that much is certain,
but you're not connecting the dots here. I'm going to have to walk

you down a different path. You can investigate all the homicides in California, and you'll never know what one of our days was like. Never!"

"Listen," Hand said, "there's no way I want to compare my life to yours. And you're right—I can never walk in your shoes. My hat's off to you and all the guys you served with, and I'm honored to have you as a relative. But we seem to be going backward. I guess it's this damn case...the Miller thing, I just don't seem to know where to go, and it's frustrating. To be honest, I'm at the end of my rope; if I can't break the case, it will probably result with the killer striking again. Then I can only hope that he fucks up, but in the meantime, I'm chopped liver. There's this one reporter for the *San Diego Union* that keeps writing articles on me and the case. Every month or so there's some other damn comment on the sensational case that's got the police buffaloed. Naturally, all the blame falls on me and my partner, Jaffe."

The wind blew through the chimes as both men waited for the other to speak. Beer was sucked from the bottles as Uncle Bill eyed his nephew, sizing up his next move.

"I think you've missed something," Bill said flatly.

"No shit," Dick responded, "so does all of Southern California, but I'm no mystic, so if you've got a fucking crystal ball, bring it out. I'm all ears!"

"There you go again," his uncle grinned.

"So you think I would do better by joining a circus and becoming a traveling gypsy," Hand responded sarcastically.

"Well, maybe you should," Bill said as he reached for the box the pictures had been kept in. "All ears," his uncle chuckled, "that's so cute, I never thought of it until now. All ears, that's great."

With a swift move that caught Dick off guard, his uncle reached for the box, hesitated for a brief second, then pulled out a string of twisted material that at first glance looked like shriveled dry prunes or dates. There were several dozen of the grotesque blackened items on the discolored loop. Dick stared for ten seconds, and reached out to feel the unrecognizable collection. They were hard to the touch, like old pieces of weathered rubber. Instinctively, without knowing for sure, Hand dropped the string and made eye contact with his uncle.

"Ears and tongues."

"What?"

"You heard me, ears and tongues. I used to have a whole lot more of them, got rid of most of my finger collection about five years ago. I started dating this woman from Dana Point, she spent a lot of time here, and I was afraid she might find my fingers, so I flushed them. Figured it might freak her out if she found a bunch of old fingers laying around the house! Not your average Martha Stewart–type home decoration would you say? Kinda sorry I did it, hell I shoulda known I wouldn't stay with the bitch...she was too young anyway. I shoulda recognized it for what it was...a good fuck, and hell, who wants to fall in love at my age? But what's the point? I mean, they're kinda hard to display in most circles...old fingers, that is. Outside of my friends I served with in Nam, you're the only one to ever see these. Sometimes I think I should get rid of them, put them down the toilet, but I can never bring myself to do it. Like I said, I got rid of most of them—shit, they'd toss me in jail forever, I mean this has got to be illegal, right? It's funny though, I really miss them, they made me feel relaxed out here on the balcony, beer in one hand...fingers in the other. Don't go telling any of your buddies on the force. Just our secret, OK?"

Dick Hand stared in stunned silence. His uncle was becoming animated and grinning broadly, as if some huge weight had been lifted.

"What's the matter...cat got your tongue?" Bill laughingly bellowed. "Oh Christ, that was great wasn't it? I didn't plan it. Hell, cat got your tongue! That's too funny! Dicky boy, this has got to stop, I'm likely to bust a gut. Jesus, cat got your tongue? I'm all ears on that one!" Tears of laughter streamed down his face.

Gradually, Bill's burst of energy subsided, and Dick Hand

knew he'd crossed a line and would have to be careful where he stepped.

"Why?" Hand asked.

"Why what?"

"Don't be cute, Uncle Bill. Why'd you do this? I mean why do you put me in this position? I'm a cop, you know!"

"So sue me...turn me in," his uncle hissed, the smile erased from his face, the expression replaced by cold eyes that pierced to the back of Hand's skull. At that moment, Dick Hand knew he was in the company of a magnificent killer. The face said it all, and at once Hand felt the shivers along his spine and was thankful he had a gun. Still, the fact that he was armed didn't make him feel safe; it was as if his uncle could kill him with looks, secrets hidden so deep that there would be no defense. A nod of the head would send the detective into orbit, and he knew then and there that no matter how long he stayed a cop, he'd never know a better killer than his uncle.

"I'm waiting." Hand spoke first.

"Pick them up," his uncle demanded. "Wear them around your neck, like the gold necklaces all these fags wear here in sunny Laguna. Pick them up, and stick your head through the center, then we'll talk."

Almost as if he were under a wicked spell, Hand reached for the knotted black body parts. He looked closer, and felt an odd sensation of revulsion and intrigue simultaneously. He pulled the string and brought the necklace close to his chest. The ears and tongues were clearly visible now, and he instinctively took a deep breath through his nose.

"They don't stink," his uncle interrupted. "Been cured for years, hell, I used to wear them around the house, then I quit. Only do it occasionally now, usually when I'm drunk. Makes me feel alive. Don't think I'm too odd, I mean lots of my buddies still have all type of souvenirs...smuggled them home, hell, it was easy. One guy I know has a matching set of skulls. They sit at each end of his couch, all varnished and shiny. People think they're fake, and he gets a big thrill out of letting guests touch them. There's more, but for now, put on my necklace. I'd be honored."

Dick bowed his head and slipped the macabre collection onto his neck, let the body parts rest on his chest, and looked directly at his uncle.

"They don't look too good on you," Bill said, "but after a while they'll feel more natural."

"This isn't natural," Hand replied, "I feel like I'm being initiated into some secret Indian society. All we need are some mushrooms, hell, I could become a perverted Carlos Castaneda. I'm sure glad you have plenty of beer. So what's next? Assemble your own human? Got a kit handy? Jeffrey Dahmer, where are you?"

His uncle tilted back in his chair, rocked on the two rear legs, and smiled. His fingers laced together across his stomach as the odd game of intrigue and suspense continued. It seemed an eternity before Bill said, "Let's walk around the deck, get a better look at the ocean."

As he rose, Hand felt the weight of the human appendages as he bowed forward and pushed back his chair. When he stood upright the necklace hit him on the chest. He thought to himself that he wished he'd worn a T-shirt rather than the open neck shirt he had on. That way the decayed parts wouldn't touch his skin. But it was too late, and for the first time he realized that he was totally under his uncle's control. He looked down at the bizarre collection and noticed that some of the parts were considerably longer than others.

"Why are some of these tongues so long?" he asked, trying to be casual. They stopped and leaned against the balcony railing and gazed out over the ocean. Hand was glad he could bend forward, leaving the parts to dangle over the side of the enclosure.

"Oh, those. Those are fingers...all I've got left, like I said... Hell, there's a real smorgasbord of parts there. I used to have..."

"I get the picture," Hand said, "but I sure as hell hope there's a reason for all this crap. I mean it's not every day a guy adorns himself in human body parts, and I still don't see how all this is going to help me...or you."

"The dinks used to cut off our guys' dicks. Slice off American balls and penises and stick them in the troops' mouths. The men were still alive. Gooks would sew their lips around the dick and the guy would suffocate on his own cock. How about that? Dear mom and dad, your son died while eating his own cock! Can you imagine? We turned bad; who wouldn't? You can never come home from that, Dicky boy, and hell, in a very real way, I miss it. I'd go tomorrow but I'm too old and what would it matter? Really, I think it's all I ever knew." Bill drew a deep breath and continued.

"I don't belong here. Not just here, but everywhere." His uncle turned and opened his arms, displaying a one-hundred-eighty-degree turn from shore to shore. "I shoulda never come back to the States, the real world for me is where those tongues came from, somehow the return never fit. Nam's my world."

"Well," Hand replied, "if it makes you feel any better, I *sure as hell* don't belong here either, but probably for a different reason. I mean, walking around with body parts draped from my neck makes me think something is awful goofy. You know, I've never much thought about it, but yeah, having human parts as part of your apartment furnishings is probably illegal. Doesn't it strike you as odd? Shit, this is nuts!"

"Not really," his uncle replied. "Some people collect rocks or paintings, and hell, it's not like I still go out and harvest the parts. It's just part of what I am...of who we were. In your world, it's queer as hell. But for me, it's a connection I'm afraid of losing. A part of my past that I live with every day, and without it, I'd feel lost. You'll never know, so what's the point?"

Dick Hand spoke. "You got it. What's the point? Maybe these things give you some vicarious strength. Make you feel young, or something, but for me..." his voice trailed off. He turned to his uncle and incredulously said, "And I don't think comparing your collection to your neighbors' agate garden or tomato plants is a fair offering. Have you ever thought that this is nuts? Actually crazy? Really, you'd be thrown in a mental hospital for this shit."

A long pause hung in the air. Uncle Bill did not answer his nephew, for at that point there was no amount of talk that would span the breach of time and experience; Viet Nam had changed all that. Bill could never go home, and Dick Hand would never fully understand any of the haunted experiences of his uncle. No one could.

After a period, his uncle spoke. His voice was slow and deliberate. "Your dead guy. The stock broker...he was a Marine, right? Served in Viet Nam. He was a grunt...combat infantry, tour with ninth Marines in '67, ain't that correct?"

"Yeah, but that was over thirty years ago, and besides, I checked his military record, it's spotless. I see where you're going with this, but it just isn't there. Got to be some other link, something more current...or it was a mistake, poor bastard in the wrong place at the wrong time."

"Give me my necklace," his uncle said.

"Gladly, I wasn't really bonding with it anyway. Hope that didn't disappoint you," Hand quipped and bent forward. He quickly removed the human remains and handed them to Bill.

His uncle carefully received the macabre items and slowly turned them in his grasp. Bill touched them almost kindly, as a jeweler would handle precious stones. Dick watched as his uncle delicately fondled the blackened flesh, then Bill jerked upright and looked directly at Hand.

"Ears are your answer, Dicky boy! I thought you were smarter than this, but maybe I took the wrong approach. My necklace was supposed to open your eyes...but I guess you saw the wrong thing. In fairness, I should have been a little more gentle, but that's all history." Bill caught his breath. "How far back did you dig?"

"Like I said, far enough to know this guy was a good Marine and there's nothing odd about any of it. Shit, I've looked at his grade school report cards for Christ's sake— don't think I'm a total dumb shit just because I don't wear body parts to a party!"

"Like I said, Detective," Bill toiled slowly and forcefully, "look to the ears, I got a feel for this. I'm just trying to help. But that's something you need to look at from another angle. How many other murders have had the same M.O.? I mean, have the missing ears?"

"None," Hand replied, "you think I wouldn't know?"

Bill walked to the table and placed his necklace back in his old box. He sat down, and motioned for Hand to do the same.

"Do you have the ability to look at homicides nationwide?" his uncle asked.

"Yeah, sure, we have these marvelous machines Bill...they're called computers," Hand replied sarcastically.

"Have you done it, smart ass?"

"No, not exactly. I mean, I know all the murders in this area for the last eight years, I'd know if there was a connection. Give me some credit!"

"Ears. Have you referenced ears?" Bill looked directly into his nephew's eyes, and knew at once he'd ignited a spark, "with those marvelous machines you call computers," his uncle allowed the cynicism to sink in for five seconds.

"No," Dick Hand replied, as his brain began to register what his uncle had been saying. How easy, and simple. Did he just not think of it? He rose from the table and paced. Like a surrealistic and grotesque fantasy, a picture of the obvious immediately took form in his mind. Thoughts came at a quickened speed, as a different mosaic emerged. At once, he felt the urge to run to the San Diego police station and access the information before anyone else stumbled upon the same thought. There were no guarantees—it could be another dead end—but instinctively he knew, deep in his soul, that his uncle was right. "Jesus fucking Christ," Hand said out loud to no one. "Christ, damn it," he nearly shouted, as he picked up the collection of tongues and ears and replaced them around his neck.

The new San Diego police station was a marvel of efficiency. State of the art. The computer room was staffed twenty-four hours a day. Hand was computer literate, but no geek. He hoped that he had the ability to access the information he needed without attracting attention or having to ask for help. This was going to be his baby, and he wanted to be as inconspicuous as possible. Several officers said their required hellos, but fortunately none of them stopped to shoot the breeze. He quickly got into the file he needed after registering his badge number and secret PIN identity.

Murders. All states, nationwide. The last two years. The computer was quick, the giant H.P. mainframe filling the screen with hundreds of names. *A process of elimination*, Hand thought to himself. *Males, segregate by males*; he gave the command to the computer. The screen reacted, and in thirty seconds the monitor had purged all the female homicide victims from the report.

"Unsolved or open cases," Hand typed in and hit the return. Nearly two minutes passed as he nervously looked over his shoulder, feeling the excitement build as the list was narrowed to less than two hundred dead men. All the list did was to reveal names, dates, and locations. Hand stopped and tried to think of how to narrow the list further. What information should he input? He tried "ears."

Nothing. The computer simply stated that it did not recognize that prompt, punctuated a large question mark, and asked Hand to enter another command.

"Mutilation," he entered, as the machine seemed to take on a pulse of its own. An agonizing period passed, then the screen showed eighteen murders over the last two years where the victim had been mutilated. The mutilations did not reveal specifics; he needed ears and not homicidal axe-murder victims. Detective Hand tried several other commands to try and narrow the search.

Each prompt came back with an "Information not available" state- ment. A dead end.

Hand entered the command for victim backgrounds, which then listed hundreds of options. Hand studied the groupings to try and determine which category would best suit his inquiry.

"Military," he entered. Within seconds it was revealed that nine of the dead men had a military background. "USMC," was entered, and the list narrowed to four men. Hand sat back and took a breath. For the first time he felt the sweat run down his face. "Names," was entered next. Then "dates" of deaths, as well as enlisted time in the Corps. His man, Danny Miller, appeared; the other three names he did not recognize. Hand knew he was close. "Service in Viet Nam" was entered. All four men had served in Viet Nam with the Marines, but no dates or military units were in the database. "Shit," Hand thought to himself, as he printed out the names of the dead men. He shut down the computer and headed out the door for Camp Pendleton.

The major at the huge base archives and records facility was more inquiring than Hand thought he should be, but still, his help was needed, and so Dick put on his best face. Hand gave him the list as he sipped a cup of coffee and looked at the office. It was clut- tered with Marine Corps memorabilia of every description. The major looked over the list and glanced at the detective.

"Ever been in the Corps?" the major asked. Hand could tell by the voice that it wasn't really a question, but if he answered no, the officer would be more condescending. Still, he had no choice; he couldn't bullshit his way through this one. "No," Hand replied, "but I'm certain the Marines are the finest soldiers in the world," he quipped, hoping to get on the major's good side.

"Marines aren't soldiers, Detective. The Army fields soldiers... and there's a difference—it would take ten good doggies to make one poor Marine. The Corps produces Marines, and they sure as hell can't be compared to that rabble the Army shits out...soldiers!

What did these men do? These guys you're looking for? You sure they're all Marines?"

Hand was feeling pissed, but he knew there was no argument he could use to win this conversation deep inside the Marine base at Pendleton. "Nothing's for sure, Major," Hand replied, "they're all dead men, and I think the Marine Corps might be the thread that ties the cases together. These men are all near the same age, all served in Viet Nam, all were mutilated, and are all ex-Marines."

The major sat for several seconds before answering in a stern voice. "There are no ex-Marines, Detective, only former Marines."

"Fine," Dick said. "Listen, I'm really not prepared for a brief history of Marine Corps folklore, I just need to find out more about these men. Can you help me?"

"Maybe...we'll see. Do you have serial numbers on these guys? When these men enlisted, we didn't use social security numbers, the Corps had its own numeric classifications. As far as I'm concerned, it was better than the current system, more distinctive of the Corps."

"No serial numbers, but I've got lots of background information. The fact that they were all in Viet Nam is a link I'd like to pursue, but the information in the police data base only goes so far. So if it's not too much trouble, can we proceed?"

"Yeah, but I'm not sure what you expect to find," the major droned, "I mean, it's not real unusual that men who enlisted in 1966 were in Viet Nam. Hell, everyone went, it was a bad time, but the Corps showed its character...highest body counts of the war." The major put on a set of reading glasses and began to enter the men's names. "Always like to help the police," he said in a voice that was less than convincing.

As he passed down the list of names, his facial expression didn't change. Because of the names, years, and dates, it was easy to group the dead men in an identifiable category. As the major continued, his only comment was: "interesting."

"Well, I think I have what you're looking for," the major said at last. "All of your guys served in the same unit in Viet Nam. Ninth Marines. That means they were all 0311s, grunts, combat infantry—and believe me, they all saw some heavy fighting. It was a long time before I joined the Corps, but the history of One Nine is legendary. These guys always stepped in the shit. Rumor has it that the unit was jinxed; everywhere they went they caught hell. Good Marines, but something went wrong; they were known for mutilating the gooks, taking body parts of every type. Well, the dinks weren't stupid, I mean they retaliated, and every time the Ninth left the parameter, the V.C. followed them...hounded the unit: booby traps, ambushes, and snipers. The men died like flies, and the corpses all had the death card in place."

"What the hell do you mean, 'death card'" Hand said.

"Ace of spades, Detective...you never heard of it? The card of death."

"No, I'm afraid not, but then I was never in the Corps, as you know."

"The truth is, Mr. Hand, I've never been in combat—just bad timing I guess—but what these guys went through is almost unbelievable. Part of the daily experience was to have the dead Marines marked with the ace of spades. Was supposed to add a more sinister side to the man's death. PsyOps, Detective, means psychological operations; we still use it, but it went crazy in Viet Nam. I guess there were no rules, and the ace of spades was just one way of sending a message. It was used by the gooks, I don't know why, but that particular card was the face of death, and 1/9 came upon it more often than most. The notion of the ace of spades and death probably originated some other time, but it was a calling card in Viet Nam...kind of a rubbing of salt in the wound. But like I said, I wasn't there; I just know the rumors. I have no idea where it came from, but I hear it sent terror through the ranks of the Marines. Anyway, your guys all served in that unit, and I'm not a detective, but it seems obvious to me that four dead guys in four months with no other connection...ears cut off...well, the answer is in front of you. But hell, it still frosts me to think this could be the work of other Marines."

"Let's see if we can get some further information, Major," Hand said. "Can you pull up a roster of men who were with One Nine in that summer...1967?"

"Here we go," the major said.

Hand waited for an eternity; he knew he was close to his answer, but the trail was so old. Trying to sort out personalities from thirty years ago was difficult—especially when four of them were now dead.

The major was beginning to impress Hand. After five minutes he came up with what seemed the best of all possible directions.

"Detective," he said as he pulled a single sheet of paper from his printer, "if there exists an objective person from that long-ago summer, it probably is not one of the combat Marines from the unit. It's got to be someone else. Lots of these guys were killed outright before they left Viet Nam, others would rather forget, but here's your list."

"Well, Major, I'm lost. If not men who were in the unit on a daily basis, side by side, who else would it be? I mean, we can't dial in mystics or aliens, so who else is left? The connection is here, with their old unit—why wouldn't they be the ones to ask? So I must confess ignorance; I'm not a Marine, never have been, so clue me in...who would that mystery man be?"

"The unit took lots of casualties, over 70 percent, month in month out." The major's voice turned friendly. "Find the corpsman...the medic. They were Navy medical men attached to the units. They went with the Marines into the field. Their casualty rate was actually higher than the grunts, but if I were a betting man, I'd say that this guy, Doc Wood, could help you out. Wood was with the unit all during this time, so if he's still alive, I'd try and find him."

"What do you mean *if*?" Hand asked. "What do you know about him? He's still alive, right?"

"He lost a leg during Tet, 1968. The only records I have are of his time with the unit, but if I were looking for a clue, I'd say he would remember what was going on and who you should be looking for...shit, he was the glue that held the Ninth together."

"Where would I go?" Hand felt as if he were now being spoon-fed by the major. Out of control and in a foreign land.

"The V. A., Detective. Check out the Veterans Administration. The guy, this Doc Wood, will have an extensive record in the V.A., he's a ward for life, has to have permanent disability...his leg was blown off, and if he's still alive, he might be able to tell you where to look. But, hell, I have no way of knowing if he's still sucking air or been in the dirt for years...that's your job."

Hand gathered up his notes and shook the major's hand. There was little time for further talk; time was spinning wildly, and Hand's brain was on the verge of explosion.

The Veterans Administration records confirmed that Doc Wood was very much alive. A file on the aging corpsman was sent to the San Diego V.A. at the east end of Mission Valley. Hand paced the floor, waiting for the information from the man that would cement his case. The record was not revealing in any way. Doc Wood was living in Texas, and as it turned out, was employed by the very Veterans Administration that cared for him. He had worn three different prostheses over the last thirty years, each one better than the last. His counseling for PTSD continued through support groups that met twice a month at the V.A., and for all practical purposes, the medical man was doing as well as he could. The report was very objective, and offered no information—other than the man's address—that could be of any use to Hand. Dick phoned Jaffe and told him what he'd found. They exchanged vows of silence, not wanting anyone to know what new information had been gleaned in the last few days. A nervous explanation of why he'd have to go immediately to Dallas was produced for Captain Del Vecci and

Dick's wife. By eight the next morning Detective Dick Hand was flying east, talking to nobody, and scribbling notes to himself.

Routine inquiries led Hand directly to the V.A.'s administrative offices where Doc Wood resided as a senior case worker. Arriving at twelve thirty, the detective showed his badge, and was ushered into a small cubicle and told that Wood probably was in the cafeteria for his morning coffee or lunch. He would wait. There was no hurry. He folded his coat over his legs and sat in a stiff metal chair. He looked around the little room and saw all types of military-related posters and decorations, different awards that Wood had gathered as a civil servant. Two pictures behind his desk caught Hand's attention. The grainy eight-by-ten photos included fifteen to twenty people, obviously military men, smiling and posing for a staged snapshot. Viet Nam. That was apparent: the jungle utilities, M-16s, blank stares, and a look of absolute loneliness. Hand was focusing on the pictures when a voice caught him by surprise.

"1967, Detective...Ninth Marines," Doc Wood entered the tight space carrying coffee in one hand, "one of the best group of killers that ever donned the uniform. Fine men I was privileged to serve with. I sewed up most of them, and like to think I saved several of their lives. We were tight—a bond that's hard to describe—but that was a long time ago, and so not much to dwell on unless you come to my PTSD meetings. But I can tell that you're way too young to join, so to what do I owe this special visit...the receptionist tells me you're all the way from San Diego?"

"Just some routine questions, Mr. Wood. A major at Camp Pendleton recommended me to you. I'm working on a series of ugly homicides, and the trail leads to the unit 1/9 because all the dead guys served in that unit at the same time...and that's the only connecting factor. Before I go too much further, I hope you know that this conversation is private, and after reading your military records, I believe I can trust you to keep this meeting within these walls."

"No problem," the Doc answered.

A ten-minute synopsis ensued: names, method of death, and type of mutilation. The missing ears. Doc Wood was pacing in his cube, the rhythmical pounding of his artificial limb against the floor accelerating with Hand's weaving story.

"And so, Mr. Wood, with that information, and what you know about the unit, do you have any ideas about where I should be looking? This is the only common thread. I'm certain it's the answer to the crimes. And I think you can help. Within this unit is the key to the killer. He's part of the picture…maybe he's *in* a picture," Hand nodded his head toward the photos on the wall.

Doc Wood turned and stared for a long moment at the two pictures, then carefully pulled them both from their nailed hangers and placed them side by side on his desk. He took a Kleenex and dusted the glass surfaces, then gently ran his finger across the photos and stopped at certain individuals. Hand could hear him mumble quietly under his breath, "dead," as the medic traced the picture.

"I assume this was your squad," Hand finally broke in.

"Platoon," Doc Wood corrected. "This was our whole platoon, and half of them were too sick to be in the field. Shit, what a time."

"I'm no military man, Mr. Wood, but I know enough…I've been taught enough recently to know that a Marine Corps platoon was made up of forty to forty-five men—where are the rest of them? You don't have any idea of the crash course I've received in Marine Corps arrangements or history. Christ, I can't stand too much more of this crap, I'm not trying to enlist…just to find a killer. So, where are the other men? Do you have pictures of the rest of the platoon? If we see them all, maybe you can help in pointing out the logical candidate for the murders. I think a killer is among them."

"Oh, believe me, Detective, a killer is in *every* one of them…and a good killer."

"Mr. Wood, I don't need any more folklore of the Corps abilities in Viet Nam, the major at Pendleton gave me all that I can handle." Hand's voice expressed his frustration at being led down another path of military lecturing.

"Well then, Mr. Detective," Wood responded in an irritated voice, "with all your research and knowledge, you would have to know that the guys in this picture *are* the platoon...all that's left. And yes, Mr. Hand we *should* have been close to fifty men strong, but this was Viet Nam...and our fucking casualties were horrific... I know, *I* pieced these guys back together! The ones I couldn't fix, I got to send home in body bags. Twenty five-man platoons were common in the Corps, Detective—shit, you couldn't fill the holes fast enough, men died so fast you didn't even get to know their names. See this guy here?" Wood pushed the photo at Dick Hand.

"Yeah, of course I see him."

"Well he was Ski, that's all. Never did know his name, he was dead a couple of days after this picture was taken...Ski, not even the courtesy to know his damn name. Sap, dead...sin loi muther fucker. It still bugs me; I should have known his name." Doc Wood's voice trailed off as he took the picture back and stared at the two photos.

"O.K., Mr. Wood, maybe we should go back to square one. In the last four months, guys in this platoon who lived through Viet Nam have been killed. Their ears have been cut off, and there is no other connection with anything else in the universe besides this outfit. I was recommended to you because you were there and would have some idea of what might be going on. But shit, if you don't know any of the guys' names...I guess I'm just wasting my time and yours. It was a long shot, but I have to think that the answer to the killings is in one of those pictures. If I have to, I'll get the legal authorization to seize both of those photos and see if someone else can help me. You're not the only survivor, so maybe somebody with a better memory will come forward!" With that, Hand picked up his coat and began to walk out the door.

"Detective," the voice followed, "look for this man—his name is Rose, and if anyone had reason to grease the whole fucking platoon, it would be him. I'd be amazed if he was still alive, but if he is, he's the key to your lock." The corpsman pushed one of the photos at Hand, and pointed his finger to the slightly built man leaning against his M-16. Hand looked for ten seconds and said, "God, he looks like he's twelve years old, why would he have any reason to kill people thirty years later?"

"Sit down, Detective. Like it or not, you're going to get another dose of Viet Nam history." Hand sat, holding the photo, and listened to the sordid tale from distant jungles of a distant war. Spellbound, he didn't say a word for fifteen minutes.

"Hard to believe...incredible," Hand said when the corpsman had finished his story. "These were just kids, but if you say it's so, I have to believe you. But still, a whole platoon would set this little Jew up to die? Every one of them would have followed this Gunther guy...why?"

"Not hard to believe at all, Detective. First, it wasn't everybody—some guys didn't know a thing, others only learned of it after the fact. But it's not hard. Detective, if you'd been there, you'd know...it's not hard at all. Gunther was our Captain Ahab, our leader, and the man who would see us through until the next day. Lives were measured in minutes— one false move and you left the planet. And like most people, some of the Marines just didn't *want* to know. It was safer that way; shit, turn your head and pretend, and if you were lucky, you'd live another day. Yeah, we were kids, but if you had shared our world, you wouldn't say stupid shit like...'hard to believe.' Gunther was good, and in that setting, a God. Gunther was law, and if he said Rose needed to go... nobody questioned it. Not a second thought. Guys died or were terribly wounded most every day. Their lives changed for all kinds of different reasons. It was as easy as being told to build a fire—you just did it. Only problem was that the dinks didn't do their job. Somehow Rose lived, and I'm responsible for that. I could've let him die, but shit, I didn't know he was marked for death...it was after, just like I told you, in the dark...the guy—I still don't know who it was—spilled his guts. Later, in the V.A., I saw Rose. What a surprise, I thought for sure he'd be dead...hell, he should've died, but I told him what I knew, and never heard from him again. Is Gunther alive?"

"I guess," Hand said. "I haven't looked him up, but he sure isn't one of the dead ones." He pushed a piece of paper across Wood's desk.

The Doc shook his head and sighed. "That's them? All dead?" he asked.

"Yep, but no Gunther, and so as long as I'm here, would it be too much trouble to access information on both Rose and Gunther? I mean this is the V.A., so chances are there's a paper trail."

"Shit," the Doc mumbled, "best put down your coat again. Let's see what we can find."

He put on a pair of glasses, and sat at his computer. From the other side of the desk, Hand heard only faint grunts and sighs, as fingers ran across a keyboard.

"There he is," the Doc spoke. "I figured that, with his injuries, he'd have to be in the V.A. system. Shit, I actually thought he'd have died years ago, but let's see what we've got." A few minutes passed.

"And Gunther?" Hand queried.

"One at a time, Detective...but look at this. No, stay seated, here's the tale of the tape."

Dick Hand squirmed in his chair; he was close now, and his excitement grew as each button on the keyboard was accessed.

"Come around, Detective, let's look at this at the same time... after all, I'm no policeman, but even a lowly V.A. administrator can see a pattern."

Hand was behind his back in seconds.

"Rose has been treated in a V.A. facility in New York since he was discharged from the Corps. Looks like a city facility, probably close to his house or work, I don't know, I've never been to New York. His condition deteriorated quickly over the last two years. I won't bore you with medical terminology, but his condition is fatal. Rose will die soon. He left the state about five months ago, and was treated at V.A. facilities in Florida, New Mexico, San Diego, and, recently, in Portland, Oregon. He's been on a trip, that's for sure, but after that, I don't know, hell, he may just want to see the states before he dies. What I do know is that his condition is fading fast, and the last stop he made, in Portland, the attending doctor recommended that he enter the hospital immediately...and he refused. The notes say that Rose was hostile and belligerent, and left the facility without any medications and in a great deal of pain."

Hand was staring at the papers in his folder. As he flipped quickly through the information, he stopped and looked straight ahead. "Shit, that's him. Has to be, a third-grade kid, or a Girl Scout can tie the dead men to his route. Don't need a detective for that to be obvious! It's him, the last guy killed, Keen was in Portland...let's see, according to your information here, shit, within two days of Rose's visit to the V.A. That's my guy, a little crippled Jewish accountant. OK, now Gunther, where is he?"

"Bingo," the Doc jumped after a few minutes. "Living north of Portland, in Vancouver, Washington—I think it's just across the river. I wonder, with him and Gunther now so close, if they'll ever get together for old time sake? God, what a party that would be, glad I will never attend. He's been in the V.A. also; Gunther's got 20 percent disability for wounds suffered, and 100 percent for being crazy."

"What does that mean?" Hand said.

"PTSD, Detective. I've got it too. Post-Traumatic Stress Disorder, ever heard of it? In the past it's been called shell shock, or sometimes battle fatigue, but for those of us from Viet Nam, it's simply PTSD...a term that categorizes us all as especially goofy."

"Yeah, all the time; shit, my uncle has been treated, he's nutty as a loon, still wears a necklace of tongues and ears around his house! How's that for PTSD doctor?"

"Not too uncommon, I'm afraid," Wood answered.

"Shit, oh dear," Hand placed his head in his palms.

"Let's see, Detective. Gunther is supposed to go to meetings, but he does so on a hit and miss basis." Doc Wood peered into the screen. "He's still active, and other than a foot shattered by an AK round, and being nuts, seems in good health. That's about all I can tell from this information, but you'd probably want to get to Vancouver and see what you can find. I mean, if Rose dusted Keen in Portland, and Gunther's in Vancouver...how far can that be? Ten miles? I don't know that area, but it seems like the two cities won't be far apart. Gunther would be the feather in Rose's cap...he's the real prize, he's the reason that Rose has taken this path."

"Can I use your phone?" Hand asked the V.A. man. "It's long distance, but the city of San Diego will pay."

"Be my guest."

Hand immediately called the San Diego police station, and after identifying himself, waited for five minutes, got an answer, and waited to spill his guts.

"Jaffe," the voice said.

"Lew, this is Hand, and we've got to get to Portland, Oregon... now. I don't have time to explain everything, but I've got this whole Danny Miller, ear-slicing shit figured. Call me at this number when you get your flight secured...and don't wait. I'll be here for an hour...hurry."

For an hour and a half, Hand sat and ingested the information that was shared by Doc Wood. Jaffe had called, and the two had coordinated their arrival in Portland; they would meet there at seven o'clock. As the pieces fell into place, Hand knew that he had to get to the Pacific Northwest immediately. He was certain that Gunther's life was in danger, and while he could empathize with Rose, whatever happened thirty years ago was not his area of jurisdiction. What he did know was that people were dying and that it was his job to stop it.

"Thanks for all you've done." Dick Hand shook the hand of the Navy Corpsman. "You've been a huge help. I'd like to tell your supervisor how much, but I don't have time."

"You're welcome, Detective," Wood answered, "and be careful. Gunther is a handful…I mean it, he's unreal. Rose won't stand a chance."

Hand paused for a moment, "Mr. Wood," he said, "Gunther is over fifty years old—we'll take care of him. You act as if he's some sort of supernatural deity, but this is my area of expertise, and this Gunther guy ain't gonna stop the wheels of justice."

"Well, Detective, we'll see about that, but I think you're in for a life-changing experience…and best of luck." Doc's words seemed out of place, but Hand dismissed it to his not understanding police work.

Hand's arrival in Portland was uneventful. With the exception of the construction that interrupted traffic, there was nothing unusual about the airport. His flight landed an hour before Jaffe's, so after getting his bags and securing a rental car, he went to a small bar and ordered a beer. San Diego police, in conjunction with Vancouver authorities, had confirmed Gunther's address, found his work, and even confirmed his license plate. The only question that was going through Hand's mind was how would he initiate a conversation with Gunther? He sarcastically thought to himself how he would introduce the reason for his trip to Vancouver. "Hi, I'm Dick Hand from the San Diego Police Department, and I know you had Rose set up to die over thirty years ago, and that's out of my territory, but he's now out to kill you and I'm here to save your life." Who would fall for that? Before he could organize his thoughts, it was time to meet Jaffe's plane, so the plan of action would have to be developed between the two of them as they drove north from Portland.

"You've got to be kidding me," Jaffe said, "a crippled little Jew is cutting a path from the east coast to here, wiping out people he thinks are responsible for injuries he got in Viet Nam? Maybe I can get to the bottom of this accountant's dilemma...after all, I'm Jewish on my dad's side, so there must be some shared heritage and history there, you know, one Jew to another. I wonder why the guy, why Rose wanted to go into the Marine Corps anyway? Sounds like he could have avoided the whole thing if he'd wanted to stay out of the fight."

Hand thought for a moment as he drove the rental car over the Columbia River. He knew Jaffe was Jewish, but never considered it in any of his assignments, nor had they ever discussed the fact. Whatever the case, Jaffe was Jewish in name only; Hand doubted he could even spell *Torah*, let alone preach its contents.

Jaffe broke the silence. "Jesus, if he does this to his fellow Marines, what's he gonna do to the North Vietnamese troops who shot him up? I mean we better stop this before he applies for a passport...shit, the war may start up all over again. Think of it, I can see the headlines, *One Marine Takes Out Vietnamese Family, Troops Are Called*, and the whole thing flares up again. I hear you can get almost anything you want in Saigon for cheap, maybe we could enlist."

"Our ass is on the line, cut the shit. This ain't about being Jewish, or Marines, or aging Vietnamese warriors. This is a man who's going to die soon anyway...he has nothing to live for, except to kill as many men as possible, men he believes are responsible for all the misery in his life. He may be right about the men involved, I think they set him up for death, but that's not our concern. Probably more than one side to the story, but I don't think we have the luxury of sorting all the details right now. Time won't wait, and we've got to move faster than Rose. One, we have citizens to protect, and on a more personal note, our fucking future is in the balance...I mean, how long have we been chasing this fucking

Kike? We're the laughing stock of the SDPD, and don't think for a minute that this case can't make or break a career."

"So, do we have a plan? Or are we just headed to this guy Gunther's house and catching him up on thirty years of dirty laundry?" Jaffe was still for twenty seconds; he didn't want to push Hand, for he knew his partner had an idea of what was to follow. "Come on," he said, "this isn't 'Pin the Tail on the Donkey.'" He noticed Hand's nostrils flair as he exhaled.

"We'll have to see the situation when we arrive, talk to the local cops and try and get an idea of where to start. Ideally, we just tackle this little Jew and bring him to San Diego. But, if the judge hasn't issued a warrant by the time we arrive, or if we can't find Rose, we just wait near Gunther and hope to ambush the shooter before he gets a chance to kill him. We have to capture the guy, I mean I'm certain he's our man, but the evidence is all conjecture. Although we've got DNA from the last killing, blood and piss that I'm sure belong to Rose, it'll take a few weeks to get it back from the lab; then we have to have Rose in custody to do a comparison." Hand was quiet, for both of the policemen knew his response wasn't an answer to the question asked. There was no answer, but the picture had to be painted fast. At once, Jaffe felt like one of the Earps walking to the OK Corral.

Jaffe thumbed through the folder as the car moved north. More questions were coming from his mouth when Hand raised his arm to signal a time for silence.

"You're asking questions I can't answer," Hand finally snorted. "We're entering a netherworld neither of us can comprehend. Shit, you should spend a few hours with my uncle...it's just really odd. We'll never be able to understand who they were or what they did. Nam sapped the energy out of an entire generation, and all we're left with is to catch a killer. But the more I know, the more I think the psychological blanket is too deep, we'll never penetrate. I think some of these guys just operate in a different world...they're here with us, but the distance between them and us is too great. I asked myself the same questions you came up with. There are no answers, and the further you dig, the less you want to know. For now, we have to stop a murder."

"Have the local cops been told we're coming?"

"Yeah, and they've agreed to help but stay out of the way. They don't really know squat about the situation, so the less we tell them, the better. Too many chiefs...you know...and if they smell a good PR win, it's likely they'll set us up handing out traffic tickets as police trainees when the Vancouver cops catch Rose, go national, and get all the credit. Then they'll be given some presidential medal. Our names will never appear."

"Lists Gunther's occupation as 'self-employed'—what does that mean? Any idea what he does?" Jaffe waited for a reply as they moved through the northwest corridor toward their appointment with destiny.

"Nope," Hand answered, "I haven't had time to look into much of anything, but I'm sure that our killer is close to Gunther, and that's all I know. Hell, if it hadn't been for the corpsman, this Doc Wood, we'd be looking at another dead body, I mean this Gunther guy can't have any idea he's a target, and Rose will finish him off... bang dead. The Jew is close to dying himself, so I doubt he gives a shit about much of anything." Hand's voice trailed off as he began to rethink the whole scenario. Chasing thirty-year-old ghosts. Then he closed it all out and hoped they were on the right path. What if Doc Wood had it wrong? Too many options to contemplate. He had to focus on the here and now.

"What do you think this Gunther will do when we tell him this story?" Jaffe asked as they passed a road sign indicating their turnoff was less than a mile away.

"Hell if I know, but he's probably not going to like to hear that he's being used as bait for Rose. I mean, I'd love to take this Rose alive, there's a story in here, and even though I'm confident the DNA will give us our man, a real-life confession would be nice... then the bastard can die on his own time. We can't be sure to even see Rose if we don't get Gunther's cooperation, so we'll have to lay out the story, but I doubt Gunther's going to like it; after all, it implicates him in a murder plot. Hell, if it happened the way our medical man says, there could be other dead guys that Gunther had sapped."

"Could he still be prosecuted?" Jaffe asked, looking across the seat at Hand.

"Don't think so, but hell, I'm no expert on the UCMJ, and shit, they still pull these poor Nazis out of the woodwork and deport them. Damn Germans are all eighty or ninety years old, and they still drag them in for crimes against the Jews, so maybe Gunther's got a problem. But who knows, that's probably different. In this case, most of the witnesses have been killed, the others have clouded, drug-induced memories of a time and place they'd rather forget, and the country that the crime—or alleged crime— was committed in doesn't even exist anymore. So I think that's the least of anyone's worries."

The two San Diego officers pulled over at the second off-ramp after they entered Vancouver city limits. The Thomas Brothers guide of the city had been brought from San Diego with Jaffe, and the route to Gunther's house highlighted in yellow. After a few minutes, Jaffe said, "we're about fifteen minutes away from his house; looks like it's east...almost out of the city borders."

They drove slowly and methodically toward Gunther's house, wondering, in silence, who and what they'd find. At last they pulled up on the opposite side of a non- descript, everyday-looking home in a seemingly middle-class neighborhood.

"This is going to be a weird introduction," Hand said to no one, as he gathered his briefcase and felt for his gun. "Let's go."

They crossed the street after locking the car. A neighbor, trimming his hedge, nodded at the two detectives, and eyed them with a long glance. A cat scampered past the walkway as the pair looked to their right and left, noting nothing out of the ordinary. Three steps and a cheap rod-iron railing led the officers to the door. They rang the doorbell and waited. Nothing. Some kids riding bikes passed on the sidewalk shouting something about an ugly girl.

Hand rang the bell again, but heard nothing from inside the house. He knocked on the door molding and on the screen door.

Finally, the door creaked, and a four-inch opening appeared. From behind the crack, coming from darkness, a voice was heard: "What do you want?"

"Are you Mr. Gunther? Tim Gunther?" Hand asked, as he presented his badge. "We're with the San Diego Police Department, and we have some very important questions to ask you."

There was no answer. After what seemed an eternity, Hand prompted him further, "You're not in any trouble, Mr. Gunther, but there are some disturbing events that have taken place recently, and we have good reason to think you may be in danger. Can we talk?"

"Ain't been in San Diego in years, don't know anyone there, and never been arrested in the last twelve years...not once in San Diego. You must have the wrong guy." The door stayed at the same narrow opening, as Hand cast a quick glance at Detective Jaffe.

"Mr. Gunther, if it's all the same to you, this is police business, and we need to speak. We can do it here or elsewhere, it's up to you. Again, you're not necessarily in trouble, and we're not accusing you of a thing." The implied threat of the two officers using their jurisdictional powers caused Gunther to cave in.

"Fuck it," he said, turning and walking into the dark recesses of his home.

"Listen, Tim"—for the first time Hand used Gunther's first name—"this is important, don't make it difficult too."

"The door's open," said Gunther, "what else can I do? Come on in."

Hand and Jaffe entered the house and carefully looked about the interior, but coming from the evening light to the curtain-drawn front room left them feeling blind. For the moment neither of them could see Gunther, and they both instinctively knew they were vulnerably silhouetted, perfectly framed for shooting, with the light from the outside highlighting their torsos. A reflex action caused both men's hands to move closer to their weapons, as Gunther's voice pierced the room. "That won't be necessary; if I'd wanted a firefight, you'd both be dead by now."

Sitting in a huge overstuffed chair was Gunther. As their eyes adjusted to the light, the outline of a man seemingly at complete ease came into focus. "Take a seat," Gunther motioned, "the light switch is by the door, flick it on, we don't want an accidental discharge, now do we?"

Jaffe pushed the switch, and the small front room was bathed in light. Both detectives still held their hands close to their sides; their eyes adjusted as the overhead light revealed a tidy room with a few pieces of furniture, pictures on the wall, and a fireplace mantel with a collection of what looked like withered fruit hanging off the end of the structure. Gunther sat in the recessed corner, in a chair that was aligned with the T.V. fifteen feet in front of it. "Have a seat," Gunther motioned again, but neither man moved. After an awkward moment, Gunther stood up and walked across the room; extending his right arm for a handshake, he said, "All the way from San Diego, shit, I must be real important."

Gunther's eyes were flat, gray, with no expression—it was like looking at the bottom of the ocean. He was average size, but the way he moved belied his fifty years of age. He evoked danger, and both detectives knew instinctively that this was no ordinary person. A toothy grin that was fixed and unnerving to see, gave the impression that Gunther was looking through both of them, and that he already *knew* the reason for their visit. His eyes moved between each of the officers, quick, darting, his smile seeming to say more than the men from San Diego wanted to know. As their hands touched and introductory shakes were offered, Gunther moved past them and got two chairs from the kitchen. "Sit down, Jesus, I've asked you three times, you two look like wooden Indians. I mean, it's not often I get this type of visit, and really, I've got nothing to hide, so fire away."

"OK, we'll get right to the point." Hand felt somewhat more at ease. But as he thought of an opening statement, he became confused. Where to begin? There was over thirty years of history to cover, but somehow he had to make Gunther aware of the situation, and to separate events that occurred in Viet Nam from current-day suburbia. "We believe you're in grave danger...that a man is in Vancouver, and he's here to kill you."

Gunther's grin became even wider, his eyes narrowed, and he leaned forward almost as if he welcomed the prospect of one last firefight. He looked around the room, searching for cover and concealment, and silently made notation of the locations of his various weapons. "To kill me, huh? Well, this ought to be a good tale, so let's hear it."

For fifteen virtually uninterrupted minutes, Gunther got the story, and with the exception of an occasional grunt, it was Hand who did all the talking, taking a break to sip from a bottle of water they'd bought earlier. It was warm, and gave little relief.

"So, you see, there's good reason to think you're next on Rose's list of targets, and if the information I have is correct, I can see this guy's motive for revenge. My job is not to investigate events that happened while you were in the Marine Corps, but to keep you from becoming one last casualty." Hand stopped and waited for a response.

Tim Gunther stood and paced for a full thirty seconds. He stopped directly in front of where both officers sat. "I won't be requiring your protection, Detective. Appreciate the offer, but I think I can handle this just fine. Rose is alive, huh? Well, he knocked on the wrong door over thirty years ago, and if he shows around here, the result will be very swift and certain. No cops will be needed; in the Corps we do our own laundry."

"First, you're not in the Corps anymore, Mr. Gunther, secondly, you're not in Viet Nam where you could take whatever action you deemed fit, and lastly, this is a police matter, and we'll take necessary measures to protect you and to capture a killer. That's the here and now, and you have very little choice but to cooperate, so let's make this as easy as possible." Hand was losing his patience with this entire Marine Corps vernacular, and though he respected the Corps, and the men who served, it wasn't part of his world. His world was police work, and his career was on the line.

Tim Gunther answered without really answering. "What happened in Nam is a confused matter. But, for lots of guys, the war still goes on...so I guess Rose is one of them. Fucking Doc Wood, had to be the hero. Rose should have died that day, shit, he was shot from head to foot. Damn gooks...can't trust them to do nothin' right, couldn't even kill the Jew. Shit." The fixed smile seemed to cover his whole face. Then Gunther stopped, realizing that he may be traveling down a road that could complicate his life. He moved to cover his words and confuse the picture.

"I don't know why Rose thinks I did anything, I mean there was lots of crap going on then, and the idea of removing a firing pin just seems too stupid, even for an asshole like Rose. Boy, he was fucked up, would have gotten lots of good Marines killed if he'd stayed in a line company. I really don't know *what* happened to Rose, except he ran into some gooks and they shot the shit out of him. There were odd things taking place by the minute, so I wonder why this goof ball would wait all these years to wander around the country taking cheap shots at our old friends."

Hand responded. "We're not here to try and figure out what happened over thirty years ago, that's for someone else. But it seems to me, Mr. Gunther, that from what I can gather, Rose has good reason to think you knew that *something* happened, and now in the final days of his life, he wants to settle a score. I could be totally wrong, maybe there was nothing weird, but Wood thinks there was, and if you follow the path of Rose's travels in the last couple of months...he sure thinks he was double crossed. Again, what happened then is for someone else to worry about, right now we need to keep you from dying. But shit, I'm just guessing now, I'm no attorney, but I doubt you'll have any legal problems, you're probably safe. I mean most witnesses to the event were killed before they left Viet Nam, or Rose has shortened the lives of the remaining Marines in the last few months."

Almost under his breath, Gunther mumbled, "So Rose is a killer, huh?" Then, without looking at the officers, he said, "well that might make things easier, you never know."

The police officers nodded, and went on to explain their plan to capture Rose and spare Gunther's life. Surveillance was the biggest part of the equation, and as Gunther's movements were relatively easy and predictable, the detectives felt they would be able to lure Rose into a situation that would insure success.

Certainly, Rose's standard way of killing was well established. There would be no firing from a distance, it was up close and personal...Rose wanted to have words with his victims before dispatching them with a silenced .22 caliber weapon. Probably one last reminder to men who had buried their memories decades before and who would be surprised to be carried back through all those years for a fraction of a second before losing their lives.

"We think Rose is probably in Vancouver now—he's had plenty of time to get up here from Portland. Hell, he may be outside checking the place out as we speak. He seems to know what he's doing; the other killings were well timed and meticulously carried out. If it wasn't for Rose's own bleeding this might have been a different situation, but I'm sure we have the right man. Now we need to trap him, and, in the process, save your life, Mr. Gunther."

Gunther stood up. "Rose the killer...I'll be dipped in shit." His grin seemed to belong to the Cheshire cat. He rubbed his hands as he instinctively avoided the darkened windows and moved to find advantage in his house.

"We'll be very close, especially during the night. We've already arranged to have a direct line to your phone, so you can reach us at any time...we'll only be minutes away. We want you to call us every couple of hours, and at night we'll be calling to wake you, just to see if everything's OK. We don't want any fancy stuff from you; leave your guns in their holster, if you know what I mean. We need this man alive to tie up a bunch of loose ends, and we're counting on you to help."

"I've got to defend myself, Detective—what if you're not here? What should I do, ask him to have a seat and talk over the good old days? Shit, you must think I'm nuts! First you tell me some deranged asshole is here to kill me, then you say he's got nothing to lose, he's dying anyway, then you inform me that I'm the bait, like some undercover police woman posing as a hooker out entrapping horny drunks on Friday night. Then you say not to defend myself because you're no less than a few minutes away! Jesus, who are you kidding, all you two want is a feather in your cap. Maybe a promotion! Well fuck all this shit, I'll go along, but to a point…don't expect me to walk into an ambush to further your stupid careers. You sure as shit have never been in a firefight, or you wouldn't be talking so stupid—shit, you're cops straight out of daytime T.V.!" Gunther stopped, his chest heaving.

"We hope this is all over in a few days," Jaffe chimed in, "and who knows, when it's all finished, maybe you can do book." Jaffe smiled, hoping to cut the ice that had developed in the room.

"Book my ass!" Gunther paced, eyes darting as his body seemed to transform into a dangerous animal. "You two dopes don't know shit! How many times you fired your weapon? And the target range don't count! Neither does recreational shooting on your days off… and don't tell me no deer hunting stories! Come on." Gunther was screaming now, "Shit, how many times you two been shot at?"

Both detectives said nothing, but simply looked at the man who was quickly becoming as much of an adversary as Rose.

"You know what, assholes, I've killed more people in one afternoon than you're going to arrest in the next ten years! You just don't get it! This fucker's traveled across the country through over thirty years of festering baggage, just to kill me? Well I got news for all of you. Rose was wrong to fuck with me in 1967, and not much has changed; he shows up here, he's dead! Dead! No fucking Doc Wood to help this time, just one last firefight, and that Jewish pig is gonna die for certain!"

"Well, Mr. Gunther, you do what you must, but understand with what we've heard here today, if Rose ends up dead because of your actions, there could be serious legal consequences for you. I'll stress again...you're not in Viet Nam, this is the U.S.A., and there are rules. Don't take matters into your own hands, there's no sense messing up your life now...I mean, it's Rose we want, and when this is all over, you most likely will just go on with your daily routine." Hand waited. He tried to fathom what was going on in Gunther's brain. A cop's intuition. He waited for a sign, but the mental doors closed and Hand knew he had not penetrated the armor.

Gunther sighed, "OK, let's hear your Elliott Ness idea on how to keep me alive, catch that little useless screwball Rose, and both of you be big heroes! Jesus, do you know how long it's been since I even thought of that Jewish jerk? Now this. I'm still not convinced that either of you have it right. Could be chasing ghosts, wasting your time in Vancouver while your hit man is gunning down people in Montana. Ever think of that? What if you're totally fucked up, boy won't you look great back in San Diego?"

"We'll worry about that, but thanks for your concern," Jaffe answered sarcastically. Hand rubbed his palms across his face.

After ten minutes, the loosely defined plan was laid out. Nothing elaborate, there was no time for that, and both the detectives felt certain that Rose would appear soon. He didn't have the medical option to wait. For all the police officers knew, he could well be dead in a local motel. From the reports they had received, there was very little life left in Rose's body, he'd have to act fast.

"So the *plan*," Gunther elongated the word, "let me see if I have this one straight. I'm supposed to parade around, making myself a clear target...unarmed, while you two hide in some bushes like a pair of closeted butt-fucking fags, Rose comes to kill me, and you guys pop out from cover and try and talk him out of it?" Gunther waited, rubbed his head, then broke into a huge smile and said, "God, if I'd had you two in my platoon, I'd have had both of you killed too. Christ, you're beginning to make *Rose* look good! This is some idea, I mean a group of Boy Scouts working on their first merit badge could come up with a plan like this! Are you sure you want to go through with this silly crap? Why don't you just leave it to me...I'll take care of the problem *and* make sure you two get all the credit. How's that?"

More small talk was exchanged, and after five minutes, the detectives stood to leave. "Remember, close to the phone, and watch where you go, stay very public, and call us when you suspect a thing. We will be close, and for obvious reasons, we won't be telling you our exact locations at any given moment. Any questions?"

Grinning, and dangerous, Gunther shook his head. "No questions boys, somebody's gonna die, and I haven't felt this alive for thirty years. Now I want to thank you, I like this already...Mars' last gift to an aging warrior. Let's go...lock and load."

The detectives turned and left, there was no reason to chat further. It was clear that they had more problems than catching Rose; the beast in Gunther had been awakened, and, like a bear after long winter hibernations, there was a hunger that had to be fed. It was dark when they left, and as they walked from Gunther's house, it occurred to both of them that Rose could be sitting undetected in any number of cars that lined the street.

Mark Rose double-checked his map. Homework was routine, and even with Gunther's unlisted phone number, it wasn't that hard to track him down. A simple computer and access to the V.A. personnel file gave Rose the grid coordinates he needed. He certainly was not about to knock on Gunther's door. This needed to be an ambush, and as the intended prey was the last in a short list of victims, it was to be the final act to a play that began decades ago, and was now reaching its conclusion. The aria was about to be heard.

Rose was confident. Even as the life blood drained from his body, he was certain that his trap would be a complete surprise, and that the last look in Gunther's eyes would make up for the lifetime of misery that Gunther had inflicted on him. As he drove toward the house that Gunther lived in, Rose wondered what he'd find. A crumpled old man? What if Gunther had a girlfriend? How would he handle that? Like O.J., kill them both? Well, the blood that splattered between his legs and the pain he felt from his bowels made him sure: no matter what the outcome, he'd never need Johnny Cochran to save his ass! There would be no miscarriage of justice, just satisfaction that could only be attained through complete and final revenge.

He thought of the Old Testament, and the covenant between God and man. At once he was happy to be Jewish, for he didn't have to ingest and rationalize the teachings of the Christian faith. He would live his life through the eyes of Leviticus, he would extract justice and mercy in the same way Moses was instructed to administer punishment and retribution. Morality, and the notion that killing was somehow never justified, was a New Testament idea, and a flawed one at that. Christians were wrong, the prophets from Matthew forward were weak; he had to believe this. He could kill Gunther, and when he confronted his Creator, the scripture he'd quote would justify his actions. He'd be ushered into heaven and be adorned with special favors for doing what was right. He had the quotes memorized in expectation of the divine meeting.

Inside his house, Tim Gunther worked the slide of his Ithaca .45 methodically. The throat ramp to the weapon had been shaved, ambidextrous safety installed, front and rear sites custom built, and the silver-tip hollow-point bullets fed and ejected easily from the fine-tuned handgun. Gunther went to an indoor shooting range at least twice a month...he was still an expert, and held several local titles for "combat course" records. He smiled to himself as he passed his CAR-15, loaded with a 30-round banana clip propped near his front door. He wondered, would Rose just come knock on his door? Rose wasn't supposed to know that Gunther knew anything about this, and with over thirty years of aging, Rose would assume that Gunther wouldn't know who he was, or that he was there to kill him. The juices began to flow heavily now. The killer in Gunther began to ooze to the top. He moved through the house with ease, like oil on water, quiet, smooth, looking for logical cover and concealment.

Hand called Gunther's house about eleven in the evening. "Anything unusual?" Tim Gunther had laughed to himself as he answered mockingly in cryptic military jargon, "No x-ray one, nothing to report, sorry. Have a nice beauty rest, talk in the morning. Over and out."

The night passed without incident. Unknown to Gunther, the two detectives had sat in their unmarked car less than five houses from where he lived. As the dawn approached, the weary officers drove away toward the cheap motel room they had rented for the week. They would check with Gunther again, and then try and get some sleep. It occurred to both of them that, unless Rose made his move soon, they'd either have to enlist help from the local cops, or move in with Gunther himself. Fatigue would soon take its logical toll and render the two officers less than effective. All the equations of the problem began to appear and reappear in a different order, and as Jaffe and Hand spoke to each other, it became clear that many possible scenarios for disaster had been overlooked. They would need a great deal of luck, and the more they considered, the less confident they became in their plan. Too much had been left to chance, but they were committed to the course they'd chosen, and with each passing hour, the options became fewer. They felt naked, exposed, and they began to think that the immediate task would require back-up. Each hour also brought an increasing sense of dread...the certainty that they were in over their heads. But pride and a knowledge that their careers might hinge on the outcome kept them moving forward.

They called Tim Gunther's number. No answer.

"Give it five minutes," Hand said, "he might be in the shower." Both men nervously paced the dingy motel-room floor, wondering if a gun battle was taking place right under their noses. Wouldn't they look like fools, each thought, as Hand stood and said, "Call again, this ain't gonna work."

"Hello, Gunther residence, our motto is "Suicide made possible"—may we help?"

"Gunther, where were you, we called and there was no answer?" Hand could feel his anxiety rise. "It's almost ten in the morning for Christ's sake!"

"I was out tending my garden," the cynical reply came. "Can't a guy pick tomatoes without having to ask permission? Hey, I like my garden, so what's the big deal? I've got pole beans, tomatoes, squash...hell, all kinds of stuff. Sometimes I like to just be in the garden, helps me think."

"You were told to stay in the house, asshole, now cut the crap, we don't want you out there in the open, a standing target for this little bastard to drive by and nail you. Jesus, we just went through this yesterday, can't you follow orders? I thought you were a Marine!"

With that, there was a long pause, and a reply from Gunther that was more of a snake's hiss than a human voice. Very slow and deliberate, measured words threw down the gauntlet that drained the color from Hand's face. "Now it's your turn to listen up, 'Dick in Hand,' or 'Dick Tracy,' or whoever you think you are today. I don't need your protection from this crap. I don't take orders from you, and if you think for a second that I'm gonna sit in my house and wait for some little Jewish fag to come bleeding onto my land, knock on my door, and say he's here to kill me, you must be *way* dumber than you look. Do I have to explain everything? Shit, he ain't gonna shoot at me from a passing car...hell, you already told me his M.O....right?—.22 handgun, up close and personal, probably likes to see the look on the guy's face before he pulls the trigger. Well I got news for all of you—it ain't gonna happen that way to Tim Gunther. I'm a Marine and I wash my own laundry. Follow orders! Who are you kidding? You tell me someone's here to waste my ass, and I'm supposed to follow your orders? Well, fuck you very much! You clowns, I killed more people by the time I was twenty-one than the both of you've jerked off in your whole life. Combined! And seeing the pair of you, you gotta be chokin' that chicken plenty. So, you do your job, and I'll do mine. And by the way, unless you've got a court order, keep the fuck off my property, and if you do get an order, I might just think you're Rose by mistake, so drop on by any time you want to die!"

"Settle down." Hand felt himself tremble as he lost control of the discussion. "That could be construed as threatening a police officer," he blundered.

"So sue me, jerk off, but in the meantime, stay out of my way; you knocked on the wrong door this time, Officer. Know what? You two remind me of Rose all those years ago. Inept...a pair of fish out of water...and you're gonna get people killed. Just like Rose. He would have gotten good Marines sapped, he had no business in the Nam. And you ain't got no business trying to protect me. Don't you see? With the protection that you, Rose, and your type offer...people die! This time, I could die, and it will be because of goofballs like you. Shit, you guys are way out of your league, you should be out bustin' transvestites or some such crap...so why don't you just get some sleep or read one of those Joseph Wambaugh cop stories? When this is all over, I'll tell the papers you warned me, you were a big help, and that I'd be dead if it wasn't for all your efforts. Everyone's covered. Storybook ending, you know, they lived happily ever after. You get your man...dead, you two get promotions, good headlines, and I get to keep my life!"

With that, the phone went dead. Hand turned to Jaffe and said, "We've got a problem."

Mark Rose glanced at his watch. He wondered, would Gunther be as easy as the rest? Somehow, even with all his perceived advantages, surprise being the biggest, Rose was still afraid of Gunther. He told himself quietly that there was nothing to dread—after all, he was close to death, and there was nothing more to be concerned with except one last exclamation point on his life! The final sentence. In his safe deposit box, he'd left a note. It would explain everything. He laughed to himself; maybe there would be a movie made of his sordid journey. He sincerely hoped not, thinking that the ex-wife he so completely hated would somehow get royalties out of a production. He rubbed the collection of severed ears in his trouser pocket, and thought about what the media would make of the story when it was over. Someone would piece together the puzzle, and he'd never be known as the creative accountant, but the serial killer with a purpose. Would the American people understand? Who would verify his claims? Would he be stereotyped as another Viet Nam veteran whose PTSD had finally run its course? Or would a benevolent reporter dig for details and finally come to the conclusion that Mark Rose had no choice? Would he be a huge question mark with theories about how and why he went crazy? Would he be compared to freaks ranging from Ted Bundy to Jack the Ripper? He wondered how he could have come this far, how demented his thought process had become. Sometimes he actually thought that he might wake up…that everything that was happening was a dream. The warm urine that escaped to his thigh returned him to the task at hand. Nothing else mattered at this point. The die had been cast, and there was one person left that had to be visited.

During the day, Detectives Hand and Jaffe drove past Gunther's house five times. They saw their man in his yard each time…once he waved at them without even turning to the street to see who it was. *Clairvoyant*, Hand thought to himself. *Maybe he's some sort of mystic, or does he have eyes in the back of his head?* The two men finally concluded that Gunther must have learned the sound of their engine, and was just playing games with them. Still, they didn't know for sure. All that was certain was that they were dealing with someone very different, and that he scared them both. There was something so distant and odd about Gunther that it became impossible to categorize. Nothing blatant, but the feeling that he must be some type of space alien, coming from another world, and knowing things that made this world nothing but folly. At five thirty, they went for dinner.

Mark Rose drove down "R" street only once. The house was very mundane, and the only thing that surprised him was the Jehovah's Witness building that was adjacent Gunther's property line. At first he frowned, but then realized one of his problems had been solved for him. He hadn't wanted to park directly in front of Gunther's house. He reasoned that if Gunther were outside, he'd most certainly give someone an eye who stopped at his doorstep. That could be a fatal error, for the element of surprise would be compromised. He wasn't in any shape to walk too far, and judging from the neighborhood, it seemed the kind of low- to middle-class area where residents would notice a person who didn't belong. In his condition, he'd certainly stand out. Now, for a brief moment, he'd become a Jehovah's Witness, maybe even find a *Watchtower* magazine to read with Gunther before he killed him. And if Gunther begged for forgiveness, Rose could quote the Old Testament, or some twisted statement in *Awake* to explain why Gunther's pleas were outside the Lord's scope of involvement. Maybe he could seek forgiveness when he met God. He'd have none from Rose.

While looking at the parking lot of the Witness Hall, Rose noticed movement at the side of Gunther's house. He glanced at his watch. Five after six. He pulled on the emergency brake and turned off the engine. A man emerged from within the home and stopped at the edge of the back porch. He seemed to raise his head and sniff the air, like a hunting dog seeking a scent. Although Rose's car was a hundred yards away, and no cause for alarm or even notice, the man's head lowered, and seemed to look directly at Rose. *He can't know*, Rose thought to himself, after all there'd been no one who'd caught on to his cross-country sojourn of destruction, and this man, who he assumed to be Gunther, would be caught unaware by the little man with the big score to settle. It was odd, Rose pondered, but before turning and going back inside the house, the man appeared to nod his head in the direction of Rose's car. The body disappeared behind a screen door, and Mark Rose turned on his motor and thought he'd drive a bit longer...check out the area, and wait for it to become darker. As he drove south on "R" street, he passed a white rental sedan. The occupants in the car had no clue that they'd just seen the enemy, and Rose had no idea that the officers in the bland vehicle were agents bent on his capture.

The two detectives slowed down as they cleared the side street and saw children at play and people out working in their yards. Nothing, they concluded was out of order, and certainly nothing traumatic had occurred, or the setting would not be so placid. "We'll come back after eight," Hand offered, "maybe dipshit in there will have taken some different medications, and we can talk to him."

Mark Rose couldn't believe his luck. Returning to the neighborhood, he noticed that the parking lot of the Kingdom Hall was filling with cars, as Witnesses were assembling for some sort of mid-week meeting. *Perfect cover*, he thought, his car would just blend in, and while the cult drones out their homogenized rhetoric, he could slide undetected into Gunther's yard and administer a bit of vengeance sanctified by his own Torah. He turned into the lot, stopped his car, and shut off the motor. Men in suits and women in dresses waved at him as they passed with their children, smiling and brimming with the expectation of paradise on earth. He waved and smiled back, rolling down his window to comment to a mother on how nice a girl of about four looked in her brightly colored skirt. It suddenly occurred to Rose how close to the "end time" he was, and he had to silently laugh as he thought of the "end time" elaboration and rhetoric the Witnesses used to intimidate their followers into submission.

Dressed in earthy brown and green clothes, Tim Gunther squatted in his backyard garden. He knew where Rose would pass, the route he'd have to take. It's so strange, he thought to himself, sitting there in the pole beans, setting an ambush that had been over thirty years in the waiting. Old feelings returned. He blended into the vegetation. The way the wind rustled, the smells of the plants, noise of passing cars, the neighbor's cat crossing the wood fence, stopping to look as darkness settled over the one-hundred-by-one-hundred lot. Birds sang their last songs of the day, and in the distance, shouts of young kids echoed from the street. For Tim Gunther, this was life. Focused for the kill, he realized what he'd suspected for years...that this was where he belonged, on ambush, and with each passing moment he reverted further into the life and times that had taken his youth and left him a casualty with wounds that never heal. He was on eternal patrol.

Mark Rose left his car. He carefully studied his surroundings as he nodded at several groups of smiling people who passed his auto. Rose checked his belt, felt the .22 Ruger under his shirt, and looked furtively toward the house next to the parking lot. He was certain the home belonged to Tim Gunther, but he wasn't 100 percent sure of anything. He began to have doubts. What if Gunther were on vacation? What if Rose couldn't recognize him? What if Gunther had a roommate? He glanced at his watch. Quarter to eight. Even in the crowded parking lot, Rose began to feel like a beacon, and at once he realized how differently people were dressed as they moved toward their Kingdom Hall. Sharp pain suddenly racked his intestines, and within seconds involuntary urination began. Sunlight was quickly fading as he rounded the edge of the parking lot and stopped at the cyclone fence that signaled the border of Tim Gunther's house.

In the backyard, Tim Gunther positioned himself so he would

have ideal views of both sides of his home. Anyone entering the yard would physically announce their arrival by passing into sight from either the north or south side of the building. Gunther became one with the dirt, he became part of the vines, and as he had done all those years ago in Viet Nam, he assured himself that he was invisible. His .45 had a round chamber, was cocked with the safety off. He blocked everything around him out. Everything that wasn't necessary was removed...leaving total focus.

"Well, let's get this show on the road," Jaffe said to Hand, "I'll get the tab."

"Keep the receipts, SDPD's gonna pay for this," Hand responded.

The last flicker of evening light danced in the western sky. Soft orange and amber colors lay on the landscape. The two officers started the car that would take them the ten-minute ride to Gunther's house. "I suppose we ought to sit out front of his house for a while. What do you think?"

Hand offered a calculated response. The more he thought, the more problematical combinations came into play. Like any dream sequence, the longer he dealt with the variables, the more confusing the options became. At last he spoke, "I doubt Gunther is going to shoot us...I mean, that's just Marine Corps bluster and macho. We gotta see him though, just try and get on the right page. I image he's settled down by now, so if we approach with kid gloves, he'll probably be somewhat cooperative."

"And if he isn't?"

"I don't know. But the way we've laid this out, Rose has got to show soon or we'll have to get the help of the local cops. I know we can't keep up 'round the clock surveillance with just the two of us. It'll kill us, and we'd be too ineffective to do shit within a couple of days. So let's just see if we can get a little help from Gunther, and hope we can tackle our killer without this getting out of hand. Hell, Rose could already be dead, or so damn crippled-up he can't move. His rotten carcass could be stinking up one of the rooms in *our* motel for all we know. Shit, I wish we could slow this down!"

One side of the house had a cement driveway that ran to a walkway between the house and the garage. It was on the south side of the building, and therefore Rose would have to walk the distance of the sidewalk in front of the house to reach it. As he passed the front of the home, all that was visible was a living room lamp behind a drawn curtain. He turned and moved up the driveway, not sure if he should just knock on a door or wait to see if Gunther would appear outside his home, maybe to catch some night air. Rose wanted to see the whole house; he had to know the layout of the surroundings. He had to be as prepared for anything and everything as he could. He stopped where the cement ran out, and dirt and grass signaled that he'd entered the backyard. It was too dark to see much of anything except a wooden fence, overgrown bushes, and what appeared to be a garden plot along most of the length of the rear third of the yard. He studied the setting for a full minute, then turned and backtracked down the driveway, walking to the other side of the house. No movement appeared from within the home, and there didn't seem to be any windows open. He wondered if Gunther had air conditioning, for if he didn't, the home would need circulation on this warm summer night. Should he wait?

Gunther shifted. He knew instinctively where the intruder would next appear. He'd seen the silhouette between his garage and his house. He'd watched the labored movements, studied the structure and features of the man, and was sure that it was Mark Rose, keeping the appointment to kill him. He heard the man coming around the north side of his house before he saw him. The darkened outline stopped at the corner of the home before looking from left to right, then moving into the backyard, surveying the house more than the yard. He stopped several times, and it seemed to Gunther, hidden in the recesses of the weeds and six-foot-high green beans, that now would be the ideal time to kill his prey.

Rose thought he'd go to the side door and wait. Just sit in the darkness and study the home. Look for movement. Any tell-tale evidence of Gunther's whereabouts. Shadows within the home would reveal Gunther's path and allow for actions based upon what he was to see. Mark Rose made his first steps toward the garage side of Gunther's house.

"You're looking for me." The voice from nowhere froze Rose. He stood, looking into the blackness that now engulfed the yard, waiting to hear the voice again, so as to pinpoint its origin. "Why ain't you dead?"

Rose stared hard, but the voice seemed to come from every-where and nowhere. He shivered as he realized his vulnerability, the man behind the voice could see him, and lights from the house highlighted his body. His only knowledge of the noise was in the expanse of shrubs that now menaced his fleeting existence. He'd been ambushed, that much was clear, he was once again on point, and had walked into a trap. At warp speed, Rose recalled the stark terror that Gunther had instilled in all those around him. At once, he knew that all the other killings had been mere children's warm-ups, and that now, after all this time and planning, it was Gunther who had all the aces, just as he had thirty years before. Still, with-out speaking, he moved into the yard, one slow step at a time. His physical condition would not allow for any fast reaction, so his cal-culation was to get as close as possible. He still assumed Gunther would not know the reason for the visit. After ten steps he halted.

For an eternity, Mark Rose stood silent, wondering if he'd imagined the voice that had just sent him into a time capsule of death and destruction. Gunther was that strong, Rose thought to himself, and he was forced to keep himself in the present while being overwhelmed by a flood of emotions from the dim and dis-tant past.

He moved his head from side to side, and still there was no

life to be felt, just the involuntary journey produced by an unseen power. Briefly, Rose thought of one of those alien abduction stories, for he felt helpless to control his actions.

"That's far enough, Private Rose—and don't do anything dumber that you've already done, we gotta talk before I kill you. Odd, isn't it, you come here to kill me, and really, just like before, you never had a chance." There was a rustle of bushes, and the nemesis of Rose's life appeared as if out of a dream. Two feet in front of the crippled little man was the looming figure that was the incarnate of all evil in the world. There was no urgency to his movements or to his speech, but there existed a power that defied any attempt to categorize or understand. "Well, well, so nice to see you again, Rose. Too bad we must dance the last dance at this time in our lives. If you'd had the balls to do the honorable thing thirty years ago, this wouldn't be an issue. Anyway, I hear you've been busy, killing off my old friends, sneaking up on them like the coward you always were and dusting them with that .22 I see poking out of your pants."

At once Rose understood that Gunther knew, but how? Thirty seconds passed, and Rose finally spoke. "Why? That's all I want to know, why? Why did you do that to me? Do you know what my life's been like since that day you set me up for death? There's too much to say, and too little time, but just answer me that question, why?"

In a voice that was simultaneously soothing and threatening, Gunther said, "Sit down."

"Sit down?" Rose queried. "Sit here in the dirt? You must be nuts, I'm not here to commune with nature!"

Gunther cut him short. "I know why you're here, Rose. Come closer and sit anyway, there are things we need to say, and I don't see that you're in much condition to argue." Rose's eyes followed to Gunther's waist and saw the outline of the pistol that was pointed at his stomach.

Rose squatted in the garden. To his total surprise, Gunther took a step forward and also sat down. They were no more than eighteen inches apart when Gunther took a deep breath and exhaled. "It's really not that difficult," he said, "in a nutshell, my job was to kill gooks, and protect my fellow Marines. Survival of the fittest, Rose, and you didn't fit...you were the *unfittest*, so you had to go. Darwin. It wasn't personal, I was the best at what I did, and think of it...if I wasn't, *you'd* be holding your gun on *me*, instead of me catching you with your pants down. Understand, it was a *job*; you were in the wrong place. I was a good killer, you were a fuck up. You had to go, there was no time for bullshit talk, men were dying, we had to get you out...and if it makes you feel any better, you weren't the only one who *left* for that reason. Just like changing tires, if it don't fit on the rim, the whole car gets fucked up. Tire's gotta go. No time to drive the car a hundred miles, just gotta pull over and change the flat. Desperate time, Rose...but your leaving saved a lot of good Marines!"

"Spare tire, huh? You must have been in a different Corps than I was, we were taught this term, maybe you remember it, *Semper Fidelis?*—and I don't remember thinking of my fellow Marines as tires. But you were *that* good? You could determine who was to live and die? Do you actually believe that? Shit, I was only in country nine fucking weeks! You didn't know if I was good or bad, how could you?" Rose felt his confidence build. He sensed Gunther was listening as the two aging warriors sat in the dirt.

"I have to believe it, Rose, otherwise I couldn't have lived with myself all these years. Like I said, you weren't the only one." Gunther's eyes were becoming narrow slits, and he took on a manic energy as he spoke. "It wasn't the war...hell, the war was over, the war was never to win, but nobody told us. Nobody told the Viet Cong. Come on, don't tell me you ain't heard the rumors! They've only been public knowledge for thirty damn years! Us grunts never had a chance, the whole thing was political. We weren't supposed to win no war, this was never Iwo Jima, we didn't fight until the island was secured. Most guys just did their year in country and went home. We were just meat for the machine, so I had to turn it into a game of personal conquest and survival. I knew the rules. There were no rules. I liked it, it became me. I forgot what was supposed to be right and wrong. It didn't matter, there was no law...I became the law, I was the sheriff. You know, Rose, it was the most alive I've ever been, minute to minute; I grew antennas, I became something I didn't know existed."

Rose steadied his voice and tilted his head so he could hear better from his one good ear. "So you've been guilt-ridden all this time, huh? Shit, that must be awful," Rose sneered. "Seems to me that you felt certain of what you were doing...killing gooks, killing Marines! You were God, and God doesn't make mistakes, so why feel any remorse? Just a job, right? Changing tires? So now, thirty years later, did it change anything? We lost the war, men died, lives were ruined, and we're here sitting in the dirt. Do you want me to think that you killing me would have changed anything? One thing? Did we have a better chance of winning the fucking war if assholes like you went around and chose who was supposed to live and die? I didn't die, not all the way, but I sure as hell left that country, spent the rest of my life in and out of the damn V.A. like a revolving door, and did it make any difference to history? Shit, Gunther, you were supposed to help, obviously you couldn't see the future, or maybe you haven't heard...America lost the war! Even with heroes like you, we got our ass kicked!"

Slowly Gunther spoke. "It saved lives. No it didn't win the war, civilian politicians back home lost the war. I never thought in terms of winning or losing a war. I knew what was best for my world. That little piece of the universe was my domain; I had control over it and everything in it. That was all, no *big picture,* no reshaping the make-up of the super powers, just carving a place to control. People like you never get that picture. We never fought for the country or the Corps, we fought to save our little world, and when people like you were thrown into the mix, our world became more complex. We couldn't accept that, our job was too *simple* for you to ever understand. Rose, it saved lives, and it maintained control! Hard choices were made every second, it was my world, and you were not invited. Rose, you damn idiot, you ever seen a NASCAR race? Think of it…these guys doing about two-hundred miles an hour! They don't have time to think, their world is fast and controlled. No time to ponder moves. Instinct. Don't you see, I didn't have the time to care for each person, we were moving too fast? Just like the driver of one of those stock cars, my world was narrowly defined, and I made moves that I felt would help my survival. It insured control, shit, it was powerful, I could just point my finger at something and make it disappear. A few words into a handset, and presto…whole villages were gone. Power, raw and simple. Better than the best sex, the highest high, better than being God."

"And did this magnanimous act of nobility change anything?" Rose returned to the theme as he came to understand that Gunther really *wanted* this discussion. In small increments, the two men were asking each other the same questions, and searching for identical answers. Answers that would make some sense out of all the mystery. Somehow, if they were to dig deep enough, maybe a reason for the singular moment that had so profoundly affected their lives would be revealed in one lightning-like strike. Clarity would evolve from shrouds of doubt, and some deeper meaning would allow them to put together pieces of the puzzle that had so devastated their lives. Ghosts would be exorcised and purity would fill the void. Viet Nam would have a purpose, and all that was lost there could be rationalized as if by some divine intervention; the two men could at last understand what had taken place and make peace with themselves and their last days. There would be order. Like pieces on a chess board, the players could only move into certain spots. Two and two might finally equal four. Chaos would be turned into meaning, and at this moment, they were their own best head doctors…speaking in a language only they understood.

"You think too big," Gunther replied. "It wasn't possible to think in the grand form that you're talking. We're dealing with grains of sand, bits of dirt. Minutes and seconds, not pages of books written to analyze what happened and what could be done differently. You would have never made it Rose, your thinking's wrong. It was wrong then, and you'd have gotten men killed."

"It might have been better if they had died," Rose smiled. "Then I wouldn't have had to kill them now!"

Gunther chuckled, "Well I gotta hand it to you, you're better now than you were then. But hell, these guys you been wastin' ain't had much of a chance. They didn't know you were coming."

"Gunther, I never had much of a chance either." A full minute elapsed before either man spoke.

"So now what?" Gunther's voice brought them back to Vancouver and the backyard garden that was their world. Rose didn't know the answer. He'd never considered this type of encounter, and it was clear that there were only two choices. Gunther continued. "I'll make it easier on you, Rose, because I can tell you now, you're not going to kill me. I can see your hands. There is no chance in hell that you are ever going to get the best of me, and there's no chance that you'll ever know how good I was. My .45's pointed at your gut, so there's no chance of you shooting me. So, you see, Rose, it's all about chances and choices, and I'm going to give you one last chance. I'm not a vengeful man, Rose, and I really don't give a shit about all those poor guys you been shooting, so I'll tell you now, you can just turn and walk away. No hassle, no problem."

"I can't do that, Gunther. You know I can't, and I don't believe that you really think that's an option. You'll have to come up with another idea. You see, I don't have much to lose, I'm mostly dead anyway, and given my recent travels, I think the cops will figure this out soon...so walking away ain't in the cards. But one question. How did you know? I don't believe you'd be sitting here in your garden in the dark if you hadn't known of my upcoming *visit*. So tell me how, I deserve that much."

"Boy, are you stupid," Gunther said almost sympathetically. "All you *deserve* is an easy way to exit this mess you've started up. And really, isn't that why you're really here?"

Both men heard the knock on the door. Immediately, they turned; Gunther could still see Rose's hands and look past him to the house, but he knew instinctively that the two detectives had returned to his property.

"They're here," Gunther said quietly. "Stay still, and let's see what type of cards we've been dealt. I think the *option* for both of us just made an appearance."

At once, everything that had been or ever was...changed. Instant realizations hit home like incoming mortar rounds, as the two aging Marines came to understand that this was the ending that they had both been seeking. So simple and clear, their confusion now gelled into the nutshell they sought. Rose had answered his own question, he knew it was policemen, and he knew how Gunther knew. Gunther had reached the end of his travels, and now he and Rose were tossed into an odd ending, but one that was inevitable.

Closure and finality.

The war had affected them both in ways that were clear to them, but the people who hadn't served beside them could never understand. Viet Nam was their world, and they had never been able to leave. Each day, their lives were dictated by events that had shattered their innocence in the steamy jungles and flat coastal plains of Quang Tri Provence. Their place was one the detectives could never pierce, nor understand. They were alien creatures, ripped from the body of those who hadn't walked in the shoes of the Marine grunts and suffered the unspeakable horrors that were their daily occurrences.

In incremental movements, the two had independently slid into existences dominated by the singular event in their lives. It had left them immune to all outside influence. Now, on a warm summer night, in the backyard of a quiet Vancouver residence, they were edging back to Viet Nam to seek and find the end to their twisted beginning. Speeding through the vortex of space and time, the two Marines discarded all their worldly afflictions and crouched in the dirt, waiting for one last enemy engagement. A silent pact was created, and without a word being exchanged, the two men knew that they had found a common way to leave all the pain and suffering of their war behind them. They no longer hunted or feared the other, for it was now clear that the exchange of ideas flowed by osmosis from one Marine to another. They had sought a way to end their lives, and without having to discuss what either had been thinking, the means to accomplish that end became clear. They would need no further discussion. It was over; all that was necessary was to finish the deed in a manner befitting two Marines.

As the two moved into position in the garden dirt, Gunther whispered, "Are you ready? It's time to go now, we have to go back. You with me?"

Silhouettes rounded the corner of Gunther's patio. The overhang between the garage and the house allowed light from the porches of houses across the street to filter through, outlining the bodies of the approaching men. They were too noisy, Gunther thought to himself. How many ambushes had he been on? How many years had it been? His adrenaline pumped as his nose filled with the smell of excitement. He nudged Rose, who lay flat in the dirt beside him, his silenced .22 aimed at the first enemy soldier. The silhouettes of the detectives were no longer current-day police officers. They had pith helmets and black pajamas on as they rounded the corner. The nasal, high-pitched voices of Viet Cong troops filled the brain cavities of the two men in the garden soil. For a fraction of a second that seemed a lifetime, both men thought of the oddity of their situation. They had both planned to die this night, but neither could have imagined the circumstance if they'd scripted it for each day of the last thirty years. Was it suicide? Not really, it was just *time to leave*, and the Marines knew that somehow this was the best they could do, and that they'd be ushered into warriors' company by the Valkyries in true hero style. It was their turn.

The enemy targets moved haltingly, and both men knew that it would be a quick end to the detectives if they carried through on the training they'd learned and lived by from the time they'd entered the Marines until this very moment. But that wouldn't accomplish what needed to be done, so it was Gunther that initiated the first move of the death dance.

"Hello Officers," he mockingly said. The two cops dropped in reaction, and searched the darkness for the source of the voice. They could see nothing, and they knew that they were targets lined up against the house. After a few seconds they began to relax as they assumed that this was one of Gunther's cute tricks to make them look more inept than they really were. Still, there was something different about the situation, something they could feel but could never touch.

"Gunther, cut the crap, we're liable to shoot your dumb ass for such stupid shit," Hand roared. "Get your ass over here—this your idea of a game?"

"The *game*, Officers, is over; you see, you just lost your 'Get Out of Jail Free' card, and we're gonna teach you a lesson."

The word *we're* brought ice to Hand's blood. His brain raced, as it began to concede the combinations. He was recovering when the night was cut by the voice that haunted the yard. It seemed to echo from everywhere and nowhere.

"You don't belong here, officers. It's not your world. We didn't ask you in, but you've forced yourselves into a considered place that exists for us every day, but will only last seconds for you. You crashed the party, and the club you sought to join has special requirements—and you don't fit the profile."

Hand kept trying to figure the plurals, as Gunther kept using multiples instead of singulars.

Trying to sound self-assured and poised, Hand responded.

"Come over here, Gunther, for Christ's sake, this is no game. Now quit the bullshit and get out where I can see you!"

"You're right, Detective, this is no game, now *you* come over *here* and see what we've got for you."

The detectives searched for shadows, looking for any movement that would give them direction. There was no doubting their vulnerability as they peered hard into the darkness, hoping that some sense of night vision would soon give them focus. They wondered inwardly what to do. Was Gunther nuts? Who was the "we" he referred to, and what were they walking into? They couldn't draw guns and just start shooting into a neighborhood backyard garden, and it occurred to Hand how foolish they both must look on the private property of someone's yard when Gunther had specifically told them not to return. *We can't just shoot the tomatoes or eggplant*, Hand thought. *One last try*.

"Gunther, don't do anything stupid," Hand began, but was cut off by a laser of speech.

"I wouldn't be too quick to point out who's *stupid* if I were you, Officer...after all, you're the one who's outlined in perfect posture, and my sight picture is in the middle of your chest. Now that's *stupid*!"

Seconds turn to frozen indecision, as the options narrow, and the two law enforcement men feel the air begin to exit their lungs. Breathing is labored, as their hearts try and pound out of their chests. Mouths are dry and instantly parched, as the officers search their minds for the training manual's answer to a problem that defies logic. The need to act is negated by the voice that pierces the air and sends the detectives' perilous situation into a freefall spin.

"Officers, I want you to meet Lance Corporal Mark Rose, USMC."

The instinct was to drop everything and run. Somehow, they had entered a hallucination that was taking on a life of its own so fast that neither officer had any control of the descent. If they could just start over, back out and rewind the last five minutes, do a million things different. That was not their fate, for destiny was at the doorstep, and eternity was at hand.

"We've been catching up on some long-lost stories, and the funny thing is that both of our sagas end with the same finish. Who would have guessed? But really, we don't have the time to fill in all the blanks, so thanks for showing up, and here's one for the books."

Hand started to speak; this time to the phantom that he thought was Rose. Everything moved so fast, his brain telling him he was talking to a garden, and that he'd never heard a voice other than Gunther's and if this was a trick he'd really look totally stupid. Their world narrowed down to half speed, like watching a movie frame by frame. He felt his movements get caught up in imaginary glue. His thinking stopped as the bright orange glare of the .45's muzzle-flash blinded the night. He didn't remember hearing any noise, just seeing a huge ball of flame and being lifted into the heavens by a tremendous force. He floated, and as events went into slow motion, his mind accelerated with conflicted thought. If he were dying, it wasn't bad, he felt no pain, but he wondered if he was going to land or if he had landed. *Maybe I'm already dead*, he imagined, millions of syntaxes rushing in a fraction of a second when he felt the thud as he hit the earth.

"Goddamn it." He heard Jaffe's voice and looked toward the light coming from the garden. Three small lights followed by a large glare. He had no way of knowing that he was seeing .22 caliber flashes, and the neighboring report from the barrel of the Ithaca .45. He looked to his left, saw Jaffe firing his handgun, and wondered if he was still a part of what was going on, or if he'd left the planet. Had he left the world and returned as a spectator? The yellow and orange explosions continued from the darkness of the garden, but there was now a difference.

He couldn't have known, but the bullets from the guns of the garden had shifted from the level of the detectives' legs to five feet over their heads. The impact of the projectiles could be heard as sickening splats as they hit the house above the officers. Hand was returning fire. He had no conscious thought of when he started, of chambering the 9mm round or the instinctive response to the muzzle flashes from the darkness. He just kept pulling the trigger, not knowing for how long or how many shots were fired. He pulled again and again; it seemed an eternity for him to change magazines. *How long have I been pointing an empty gun?* In a dream-drenched quasi-reality, everything was slow, moving in waist-deep water, running with nowhere to go. Just running. He fired again, and then heard Jaffe screaming "Stop!" Four more rounds left his weapon before he realized there was no return fire coming from the backyard.

Silence. Ringing in his ears, and the wonder of where he had been and what had just happened. It was as if he were being enveloped in an insulator wrap, everything closed in, and he felt like he was being delivered into a womb, a heavy sense of disappearing, until he heard the faint, distant voice of his partner. In seconds, he seemed like he was coming to the surface of water after taking a deep dive. At once he broke the invisible barrier, and his head began to clear and he tried to analyze the situation. He thought of the old science fiction movies of his youth. Had he been abducted? Where had he been taken, and was he really ever coming home again? And if he did return home, was he going to carry a secret knowledge that the aliens implanted in him? He'd gone somewhere, of that he was certain, but where it was, he had no idea.

"It's OK, we're gonna be OK." Jaffe's face appeared over his body. Hand's focus was blurred; he knew something huge had happened, but could not put together the pieces. A warm flush traveled his body as he tried to speak. Hand wasn't sure if words were coming out. Were his thoughts exiting his mouth? He could hear, but then he couldn't. *Maybe a dream,* he pondered, *maybe I'm in a dream sequence that I can't escape.* He tried again to put order to his dementia, and in what seemed an eternity, he began to hear Jaffe's voice more clearly, as the pounding echo of the firing receded in his eardrums. His head was catching up, and he thought of his brief experience as an amateur boxer, being knocked out, and coming out of the thirty-second coma, the voices, the confusion, and finally, the realization that he had been hit and not knowing where the punch had come from. Smelling salts, a trainer telling him to stay down. For the first time he noticed the warm liquid running down his face. It stung as it collected in his eye sockets. Jaffe ripped strips of material from his shirt and wrapped them around Hand's head. He heard Jaffe say that help was on the way, and he felt the tugging on his leg as his partner applied a tourniquet to a huge hole in his thigh. He didn't remember being propped up against the house.

Sirens and distant shouts punctuated his off-and-on consciousness. Floodlights, and dozens of police. Medical people came and syringes were pushed into his flesh. He felt like he was floating as he heard the words "morphine" and "shock" in the jumble of activity that surrounded him. Police uniforms and badges passed his sight. He weaved in and out of different dimensions and serenely slipped into other worlds that passed his psyche in rapid succession. He was lifted onto a gurney, and as he was led to the awaiting ambulance, his head shifted to the yard where the firing had started. It was dark, and he was left to wonder what had happened, and how all this got started. Bits and pieces. Where was his partner? Where was Gunther? And Rose? Did Rose really exist? Did *he* really exist? Fantasy, images swirled, and he passed into unconsciousness.

Jaffe appeared, using a walker. Brenda sat talking in hushed tones as Detective Hand, waking ten hours later in a hospital, began his journey to current-day awareness. He'd been shot twice. Once, a glancing blow to his scalp from a .22 bullet. Far more serious was the hole in his thigh that was the result of the .45-caliber handgun that had sent him flying in the air. A doctor emerged from behind drawn curtains and Hand learned that his injuries would not be life threatening, but his recovery time would be much longer than his partner's. Jaffe had received two wounds, both to the leg and both inflicted by .22 rounds. The injuries were superficial, and a return to work could be expected in several weeks.

"Welcome home, it's about time you woke up," Lou joked, trying to deliver some levity to Hand's first conscious moment. "We're heroes! You should see the press on this one. The assistant chief's flying in from San Diego later today. Big award for coming out of this, I guess just for being alive. Man what an ambush." Hand tried to absorb all that Jaffe was saying, but his weakened state required more rest. He kissed his wife, and drifted off. Medications and shock required more rest, and his eyes closed again. "See me in the morning," were his last words before sleep.

He woke before it was light. Where was the nurse? In the quiet of the morning he began to reconstruct what he believed had happened. There were so many unanswerable thoughts; he knew immediately that Jaffe would be necessary to get the whole picture. Rather than struggle with questions that he couldn't answer, he allowed sleep to come over him again and drifted into a refreshing three-hour nap.

When he regained consciousness again, it was nearly ten o'clock. His partner sat reading the newspaper next to his bed.

"Well, rise and shine Sleeping Beauty," Jaffe joked, and set the paper aside. "We're headline news. You gotta get up and active or I'll have to meet with all the press people and get all the credit."

Hand hesitated. "What's it say? Did they get the story right? Shit, I don't even know what the story is, fill me in."

"Gunther and Rose are dead. We won't be getting any confession from Rose, and we'll never figure out Gunther, but from all I gather it's gonna be easy to tie Rose to the nationwide killing spree. When the dust settles, there will probably be a few more bodies to add to his total, but for now it's over. We got the killer."

Hand was slow to respond. "So Rose killed Gunther? Sitting in that garden, he got the drop on Gunther and blew him away? Hard to believe."

"It's not that easy...or simple. We're still trying to sort out a bunch of crap; but no, Rose didn't walk up and shoot Gunther. The story gets weirder by the hour, and we may never know what really happened, but for you and me, we got our man, and the case is solved."

"Great," Hand sarcastically replied, "but Gunther's dead too, and *he* wasn't *our* man, so what the hell gives? If I remember correctly, we were there to save Gunther, not to get him killed. I must be missing something, this doesn't sound like any big success. Here we are in Vancouver, Washington, we both been shot, the guy we came to capture is dead, and laying next to him is the guy we came to protect...and he's dead. The only worse scenario is if we were dead, which brings up a point. Why are we alive?"

"I'm not God," Jaffe said. "I'd like to say we're alive by divine intervention, but it doesn't look like that's the case. The truth may never completely emerge, and we can only guess as to what the motives of these two guys were, but I think we'll know most of the answers in a few days. There's investigators all over the place—our guys from San Diego are here also—so we should be able to button it up quickly."

"What do you mean, *these two guys*, you make it sound like they had this planned out, they were partners of some sort. I may be screwed up on this one, but if my memory serves me well, Rose came to Vancouver to *kill* Gunther, not help him work in his vegetable garden! Give me that paper; what's the media take on this shit? Be honest, are we in trouble?" Hands' eyes riveted on the front-page headlines of the Vancouver *Columbian*.

The articles did little to put order to chaos. All that was reported was in generalities: a gun battle, police injuries, and two dead suspects. Everyone seemed to be covering their tracks, but the paper brought up several interesting questions, and at this time, there were no answers.

"San Diego brass is due here in about two hours," Jaffe said. "You need to get some rest. Your wife should be here soon, so I'll get the hell out of here and see you in the afternoon." Hand wanted to protest, his head spun with interconnecting thoughts, but he was too weak to fight, and he faded back to sleep. But his sleep brought little rest. He seemed in a constant dream world where the electrical impulses of his brain tried to find the proper order to events but there was no proper fit. Like a computer sending information in the wrong files, Hand's cerebral activities came back to him totally mixed, and as he regained consciousness, he felt further out of touch with all that had occurred.

When he woke, he recognized the police captain from San Diego talking to uniformed police from Vancouver. His eyes blinked and cleared as the officers turned and noticed his movement. Jaffe was mumbling quietly to Hand's wife in a corner of the hospital room. Captain Del Vecci walked forward and extended his arm. "Hand, good to see you, and to see you alive."

"Thanks," Hand replied, "but I'm not so sure who to really thank for being here. What the hell happened at Gunther's? I get the feeling there's more to this fiasco than meets the eye. What can you tell me?"

"Jaffe," the captain called, "come over here and join us. Pull up a chair. Mrs. Hand, will you excuse us, we have a few details to discuss, and at this point, it's for cops' ears only. It won't take too long; we'll signal you when we're through." Brenda turned and walked from the room. The expression on her face was one of frustration, for it was apparent that she hadn't expected the request. That left three Vancouver cops, the captain, and Jaffe. "Here's what we think happened," the captain said. "It's still too early to know for sure, but there's enough evidence to put the rough outline of events together."

Jaffe interrupted, "Gunther left a note, he had all this planned out, and if I *think* what happened really happened, then we're alive because Gunther didn't want us dead. I'll let the captain explain."

"OK," the San Diego man began, "Jaffe's right, Gunther left a letter, he didn't know exactly how things would develop, but he was certain that he wasn't going to let himself or Rose come out of the night alive. He'd made a pact with himself to end it all, and we think he was counting on you and Jaffe to be the executioners, but he had a back- up if that plan didn't work."

"Wait, wait." Hand extended both arms. "You're saying this was a suicide, some sort of exit that was planned from the beginning? That's nuts, I mean Gunther knew Rose was coming *soon*, but he didn't know when...nobody did. For all any of us knew, Rose could have died in some cheap motel room, or in his car. The guy from Texas, Doc Wood, said Rose was a walking dead man, so what would Gunther have done if Rose had never shown up? Sit in his garden and wait for the magic moment to blow his brains out? I'm spinning, but fill in the blanks."

"Like I said, both Rose and Gunther are dead, so we'll never know exactly what went on, especially in the time those two had together in the garden," the captain paused, "but between Gunther's note and the actual events of the night, we think that's exactly what happened. We know Rose was on a suicide mission, shit, he was near death when he arrived, and we think Gunther added up all the options, and took what he felt was the honorable way out."

"Honorable," Hand scoffed, "you call ambushing two cops honorable? That doesn't sound like the Marines' way to preserve honor and dignity, so you'll have to help me on this one too."

Jaffe spoke. "The letter makes it a lot clearer, Dick. It's not the most rational of thinking, but in Gunther's mind, his plan was to accomplish a variety of things. But what's perfectly clear is that if Gunther had wanted to kill us, he could have done that easily."

"Then why are we both shot?" Hand asked. "Do you mean that these guys were playing with us for practice?"

"Not playing exactly, but they had to do this much to connect all their convoluted dots," Jaffe responded. "Listen, Dick," he continued, "the shrinks think it has to do with this PTSD thing, the stress disorder that these deranged Viet Nam vets have. They simply don't think normal anymore. They go back and forth mentally between here-and-now and Viet Nam thirty years ago. Makes them nuts, and it makes it impossible for us to paint a real rational picture. The best we can do is to understand that their thinking is way different than any of ours...totally messed up, so the crap...the suicide Gunther pulled sounds completely crazy to us, but to them it made perfect sense. That's how different their thinking must be, that's what the doctors who know about this stuff are saying. Weird crap, we'll never know where these guys heads *really* were at...I mean, all that time in Gunther's house...hell, he must have been looking at us as the answer to his prayers."

Hand sighed deeply. "Maybe we better go back to square one," he said, "I'm totally lost. You hear of these deranged crazies that deliberately get themselves shot by cops, but I don't think Gunther fits that profile. He didn't seem unstable to me, just the opposite. He was almost pleased to hear of Rose, it seemed to make him happy...he became very calculating. Suicide by cops is one thing, but how in the hell could those two dream this up in just a few minutes?"

"Well, it probably was not formulated in that garden," Jaffe prompted. "If we have this correct, the plan was in play for years, we just happened to be the catalyst...just accidental. We were there, that's all."

"Bring me the letter," the captain said, as he turned to the ranking officer from Vancouver. The man walked to Hand and presented a folded two-page hand-written letter.

Dick Hand carefully opened the papers. The others stood silently.

> To Whom It May Concern,
>
> When you get this letter, I'll be dead. Rose will be dead. All that will be left is the story. I don't have time to fill in all the gaps. Hell, I don't know all the gaps. What I know is that the time to leave has arrived for me. If there was any doubt

about it, the information received from the two cops from San Diego was enough to insure the action.

I'm not stupid; I know what happened to Rose in Viet Nam. I also know that others now know...or think they know. Truth is, none of you will ever know what we did or how we did it. You weren't there. Still, it happened, and even if Rose is captured alive and found guilty of all the killings of our old comrades, soon after, questions will be asked, focus will be shifted to the "whys" and it will be my turn to answer. The Marine Corps has long arms and a long memory, and they may want to set the record straight even after thirty years. This will happen at my expense. I will be brought up on some charges that make me out an asshole and will glorify the Corps. At this point in my life, I'm prepared to do what's necessary to avoid this problem. I will end it all, and be glad it's over. If Rose chooses to be part of it, fine. If not, he'll be a statistic sooner than he thought.

I won't be specific, but I have no ill feelings toward the police. I know what it means to have your orders, and to carry them out. I wish the police no harm, and as you will see when my plan is carried out, the police will be made to be heroes. Everyone wins: Rose gets his death wish, the cops look like supermen, I get to leave the ghosts of many operations behind me. I also will never have to answer stupid questions about Viet Nam, and will avoid possible indictments...if and when an investigation of Rose starts, it will likely lead to other "collateral" and related incidents. I don't need that in my life. I've been considering an exit for several years, but the specter of legal action is the thing that has put the whole final dance in motion. The police will get their man...or men...and as you'll see, without me being specific, they will be award material. You'll just have to figure my meaning after the fact. So for now, goodbye.

Don't feel sorry for me, or try to understand why I'm

doing this. You'll never know. Just know it's not a difficult decision, for me it's very easy. I'll rejoin those who have gone before me, and in their company I'll find comfort.

Tim Gunther

Detective Hand paused. He turned the papers over to see if there was some further information on the back. There was none. It was as if he'd been led to the edge of a cliff and been left to make a choice: to retreat or to jump. But he knew he couldn't go forward, the leap he would have to take to enter the world of Gunther and the men like him was not one that was available to Dick Hand. There was a time portal that he suddenly felt existed, but was in a dimension that was forever outside of his grasp. Like some Super Nova or Black Hole, millions of light years into space, he could conceptualize the process, but the information overload prevented him from giving it any meaning. As the seconds ticked away, he felt himself being sucked back from Gunther's world and his words to the present-day situation that was his life.

"Some shit, huh?" the captain said. "We've all read it about a dozen times, and as best as we know...we think we've got it figured. All that's left is to answer all the questions for the press, and that part we've got to get coordinated on. Cops have got to look good, we all agree on that. Only the people in this room know of the existence of this letter. With just a little fine-tuning we can wrap this up."

"I don't get it," Hand replied. "What's to tune?"

"Here's what we think really happened. If we just drop a few minor points, it becomes a cleaner story and nobody's hurt. It's not lying really, just rearranging the sentence a little, leaving a few parts out, and making the cops look a little more polished." Captain Del Vecci turned and checked the hall door, making sure there wasn't anyone close to the room.

"Gunther and Rose had enough time to talk. In their own way, they'd concluded that the end was to occur that night. What they said, or what they did to come to this, we'll never know. Still, we think they wanted to die. Look at Gunther's letter, he obviously had no intention of walking away, and in the shape Rose was in, it must have been an easy stretch to get him to climb on board. They didn't want to kill you two—in fact, we think Gunther actually liked you, in a patronizing way. He found you funny. Kinda like the *Keystone Cops*. In his twisted mind, he was going to accomplish all things at once. He and Rose would die, and you two would be made heroes. But in a lasting testimonial, he wanted all of us to know that he and Rose could have killed you at any time. You walked into an ambush that should have meant instant death. After the initial firing, with both you and Jaffe hit and down, rounds from the guns that Rose and Gunther were firing began to hit high on the side of the house." The captain paused, and Hand was able to recall his thoughts in a millisecond, as he remembered wondering why shots were hitting above him.

"Yeah, I remember thinking that they were aiming high," Hand said. "But maybe we were hitting them with return fire? How do we know exactly what happened?"

"We don't—like I said, we're left to fill in some of the blanks— but with what happened, and looking at Gunther's letter, we think at some point after the shooting started, their plan was to spare your lives and take their own. According to Gunther's letter, this would satisfy all the angles. We do know *this* much: both Gunther and Rose had 9mm wounds, they'd been hit, but that's not what killed them. Both were killed by .45 caliber rounds, one through each man's heart."

"Jesus," Hand mumbled, "so where does this lead? If all this is true, what's the purpose of re-writing the story?"

"You're a good cop, Detective Hand, but there are things about policing that are out of your grasp. One is public relations. We're not going to look so great if everybody thinks these two guys would have killed themselves anyway, and we just got in the way. No, as it is now, if we just forget this little letter, then the picture is confusing enough to give everyone what they want. Nobody's hurt, and it makes for a tighter package. With this post-traumatic stress disorder thing in the Viet Nam vets, our job will be easier, people will just assume that the two of them snapped. Our friends here in Vancouver have spoken to the coroner, and he can help us with a few small details. In a nutshell, the final headlines will read: *One Homicidal Killer and One Suicidal Nut Killed in Gun Battle with Two Injured But Brave Cops*." Del Vecci waited for a response.

"I still don't understand why this is necessary," Hand protested, "the real story is what matters, and there could be more to this. I mean, if we'd been better prepared, maybe Gunther would be alive. Our mission was to get Rose and protect Gunther, not watch them kill each other while we provided them with good target practice. Somebody's going to ask questions, and this could get real ugly."

The captain spoke after nodding at the Vancouver cops. "This letter will disappear in a few minutes, and there will never be any trace that it ever existed. Without it, and the type of thinking that it would prompt, there is really little to get people to wonder about the situation. Yeah, there are some nagging questions, and probably some jerk-off reporter will snoop for a big kink in the deal, but without the letter, and with our tight mouths, it will always be speculation. Hell, we're still trying to find out who killed Kennedy, so do you get the picture? It's done all the time, don't worry about it, and after all, what does it matter? The case is solved, Rose is certainly our killer, you and Jaffe are poster kids for police, Gunther's an enigma, the population is safer...and who knows, maybe somebody will write a book about it...make a good mystery story."

"What if Rose or Gunther have family?" Hand still couldn't figure out the need to hide anything. "Don't you think some relatives might come forward? What if they want a real investigation? Then what?" Hand waited for a long moment.

Jaffe spoke. "In a few days we'll be in San Diego, and it will be easier to dodge questions from press people. Back home we should have a sympathetic audience, and in a few weeks it'll all die down."

"And if it doesn't?" Hand asked.

"What would be the line of questioning?" the captain queried. "The strict answer is you guys walked into the backyard looking for Gunther and the two deranged Viet Nam–era goofs opened up on you! After that it's all instinct. You don't know why or what they were thinking...they're dead. Besides, the press has acciden-tally helped us on this one for years. I mean the Viet Nam vets have always been portrayed as nuts, mental cases, baby killers, and all that crap since the damn war ended decades ago. So, why not just pick up on that theme? How can it hurt? We'll just shrug our shoulders and dismiss it as another example of that PTSD thing. Nobody gives a damn about aging Viet Nam veterans...they been tarred and feathered by the newspapers for years now, we got noth-ing to worry about. Any question you are asked can be a simple, 'I don't know'. It's not bad, really, it's just avoiding embarrassment and answering all the silly questions that reporters will ask about why we didn't take a different approach and all that crap. And hell, we really *don't* know. So get some rest, and I'll see you back in San Diego."

There was a momentary hesitation, and Hand said, "I need to talk with Lou in private, will you excuse us?"

"Of course, but remember, this is the end of the discussion. Nothing further is to be revealed...so congratulations on a job well done. I'll send in your wife."

"Give us ten minutes," Hand said.

"No, I'm sending in Brenda *now*, so you two will have to find another time to chat. Keep it vague." The captain turned and waved goodbye with Gunther's letter in his palm.

"Lou, did we really know these guys, I mean, could we have handled this differently? I'm totally confused, and all this cover-up shit...is any of it necessary? It just seems like we're setting our-selves up, and I can't see why. What do you think?"

At that moment Hand's wife entered the room. "How's my hero?" she beamed.

Jaffe turned and nodded at Mrs. Hand, "I'll leave you two alone, I got all kinds of stuff to catch up on. So, I'll see you tonight." His eyes locked onto his partner's. In a second he was gone.

"Well, Mr. Hand, this is quite a shock." Dick's wife sat on the edge of his bed. "I've thanked God enough times that you're alive, and I know how you love your work...but this is hard on me. Thank God we don't have any kids, this would be awful. Now, give me some help, what happened in that yard? Really, everyone's so *hush hush* about it, you'd think it was a national secret." She held his hand.

"I don't know," he answered, "it was all so fast, just like a car wreck, we were just part of the accident. So fast, I can't answer you, honestly, I don't remember...believe me it's nothing like the movies. The more I think about it, the less I know. Sounds stupid, but I can't give you an answer beyond what you can read in the paper, and hell, maybe they have more information than I do. I was just *there,* and after that, it's all a blur, a dream really, like trying to embrace the fog, you can see it, but try and grab it...it's always moving and changing form. It mocks your every more, shifts and disappears. It was over in seconds, I know that, but it seemed like I was slowed down to a crawl, you know, like those weird dreams that have you running in chest-deep water. But thinking of it now, it had to have been more than the shooting of bullets; it seems like kinetics, you know...the transfer of energy. Something else happened there in those few seconds, but hell if I know what it was. But, I've got to tell you, I'm in a different place. Odd, strange, I just don't know, and for now don't care to talk about it anymore. I need rest."

"I know you, Dick Hand, and there's things you're hiding, I can tell," Mrs. Hand leveled. "But we'll have plenty of time to catch up, so I'll see you later. Before I forget, I want you to know I've missed you, seems like all we talk about is this fiasco, but I want you to remember I've got plenty in store for you, it seems like years since I've had you where I really want you. I want to put on a show...and I've been practicing, so get some rest." With that, she winked and pushed her breasts together.

Hand stopped her. "It's not *hiding* really—it's just that I don't know. The more I think about it...well, it gets confusing. It's not so much the incident, the shooting, as it is the guys...those two, Gunther and Rose. All of it, the Viet Nam thing, I feel helpless, like I can't ever get into where they think. I can't help but wonder if I'd done it different, taken a different approach, maybe none of this would have happened. It's like they don't exist in this world, some-how their thought processes are so altered that we can't get in...I don't know. When we talked to Gunther, it was like he was seeing through us, he had some power that we could not share, there were simply places that Jaffe and I were not allowed. And now, now that he's dead, I almost feel like a part of him has entered me. God, it's so weird, like I've had some organ transplant from an alien crea-ture. I know it's too odd to fathom, but I'm different, like some-thing has become attached to me, a transplant or something. Scary stuff, but somehow I feel like I'm walking with them through the Viet Nam bush. Can't be, I know, but something has happened, and I can't identify what it is, or where it's taking me."

"Get some rest," Mrs. Hand admonished, "it'll all become clearer in a few days. After all, this is traumatic in more ways than physical. Just be thankful you're alive. And believe me, I've got an idea of what it will take to get your mind off some of this stuff. Me and the friend you like are waiting."

Two days had passed when Hand learned that he was to be released from the hospital and returning to San Diego. He was walking with the aid of a crutch, as doctors marveled at the recuperative power of youth. He had just finished lunch when he heard the distinct approach of footsteps. At first, he couldn't recall the rhythm, but as the noise got closer, he remembered the cadence of the artificial limb as Doc Wood entered his room.

Both men stood at odds for twenty seconds.

"I read about you in the papers," Doc Wood said, "you're on the front page around the nation. Some hero. I had to travel up here anyway, so pulled some strings to get my schedule moved around. Got to attend some regional meeting on PTSD updates. I guess I'm as qualified as any when it comes to discussing mental torment. My name hasn't appeared, but I can't help but think I was involved with this...after all, I sent you to Gunther."

"I'm leaving for San Diego in a few hours," Dick Hand replied, "I *guess* I'm glad to see you. But I don't know why you'd make a trip from Texas, the papers there will tell you the same things as the papers here, so what's the point?"

"Like I said, I had to be here anyway. Can I sit?" Doc asked.

"Be my guest," Hand answered. "I didn't think my brush with death would require your company, but as long as you're here, take a load off."

Doc Wood sat on the steel hospital chair, extending his prosthesis to take off the pressure. He looked around the room, noting the flowers and cards.

"Quite a firefight," Doc said, without looking at Hand. "You boys must have been scared shitless...and now you're heroes. What a difference a few days can make, huh? I warned you about Gunther; he was dangerous, but you guys were better, I mean the papers almost compare you and your partner to Earp and that other Doc, you know, Doc Holliday at the OK Corral. Tombstone Territory right here in Vancouver! Amazing, you walked into their ambush and still came out on top. I didn't think Gunther could ever be had like that. Not if he was eighty years old. Amazing. All that time to prepare, you two right in the killing field—must have been your superior training that compensated. And Rose, what's with that crap? Thought he was here to *kill* Gunther, not play G.I. Joe in the garden! Things must have gotten really screwed up. So what really happened?"

Hand sat on the edge of his bed realizing that the Doc was playing with him, and he wished Wood would leave his room. He knew he was being trapped, that the line of rhetoric was cynical at best, and that the man opposite him somehow *knew* that the real story was different than the press accounts. How or what Wood knew was conjecture, but Hand recognized mockery when he heard it, and determined to use the chance to rehearse his story of denial and mystery.

"Well, like the papers said," Hand began, "it was all so fast; if there are blanks to be filled in, someone else will have to do it. I don't recall; it's not like a movie."

"I know," Doc Wood replied, "and I know something else. There's more to this story, and really I don't care, but I want you to know that I *know,* and that all the posturing in the world will never get me to believe that you surprised Gunther. That simply wasn't possible, not with the information he had. I don't know, and don't want to know...but I believe that Gunther's dead because Gunther *wanted* to die. You couldn't have tricked him, he was too good."

Hand waited to form his thoughts in reply.

"You give Gunther a lot of credit. But facts are facts, he's dead and we're alive, end of story. There will never be an end to second guessing...you know, armchair quarterbacking...so what's your point?"

"My point, Detective," Wood locked eyes with Hand, "is that I'm a man who walked with Gunther, even though it was thirty years ago, I know certain things that you'll never understand. Tim Gunther was *born* to walk in the bush. He was more than a Marine; he was a spirit, like a creature that dropped from another planet, an enigma that could not be denied. He lived for the fight. I saw him work, he became one with the land. His skin absorbed the dirt, his movement blended with bending bamboo, he stood quiet on night ambush, became indistinguishable from the trees. He loved what he did, and he became part of it, he wasn't separate from the place...Viet Nam, he *was* Viet Nam: the earth, sky, mold, smells, and finally, the death that he meted out. It was him, *Viet Nam,* and there was no way of taking it out of him, or putting it in. It *was* him. There were others like him, for sure. Some people are just born for that one thing. You could feel it, it was unspoken, Gunther was the Secretariat of the jungle. He was a quarter horse of death. King of the beasts, and I don't care if Gunther was ninety years old...you would have never, never beat him on his playing field. Something else happened, I don't know what, but I know for certain that what the papers have to say makes good copy, but there are those among us who recognize a lie. You came close to Gunther's world, he allowed you to peek in then he shut the door. Be thankful Gunther didn't want you dead—it would have been *so* easy for him. You and your partner were child's play, amateurs in a sport of finality."

"Why are you here?" Hand asked.

"Just passing through, really, and like I said, I had to be in the area anyway, so thought I'd stop in and give my regards. But a funny thing happened, the more I heard of this shootout, the less believable it became. And you're right, it will never matter, and we'll never *really* know what those two talked about, so I guess I'll be on my way...and wish you all the best."

"Thanks," Hand replied, "and believe me, I never wanted to be the hero that the papers say. I was just *there* and there's not much about that I can change. I'm lucky to be alive and you're right, if things had been slightly changed, the story would have a different ending."

"I bet you just hope the ending that has surfaced *is* the ending. I mean, what do you think a good reporter would do with this?"

"I don't get you," Hand responded.

"Sure you don't, and the sooner you get out of town the better. Anyway, I guess I'm glad I helped point you in the direction of Gunther, although it certainly didn't stop anyone from getting hurt. And hell, you have to wonder what good any of it did. I think Gunther and Rose would both be gone now...even if neither one of you cops had been involved. But none of that matters, I gotta go, hope things go well for you in San Diego." Doc Wood extended his arm and they shook hands.

"Thanks again," Hand said, as his eyes traveled down the length of Wood's body. He paused at the fake leg, and said, "Yeah, I bet there's lots none of us are going to know, but then, that's life. I guess you take it where you can...give a little, get a little." He could hardly wait for the Doc to leave.

"Oh, and by the way, Detective," Doc Wood steadied himself, "don't think for a minute that Gunther's done with you. Your world will change from now on out, and Tim Gunther will take charge of most of your life."

"Like hell," Hand bellowed, "damn Gunther's dead, and so is Rose, there's not a thing I can do to change that! What the hell are you talking about? You seem to worship this Gunther guy, well, maybe for you he was a God...but for me he's just a dead Viet Nam goof! Now please leave...I need rest."

With that, Wood turned and walked from the room. At the doorway he stopped, "You've got so much to learn, Detective, I wish you luck."

Hand stayed still until he could no longer hear the thumping prosthesis in the corridor.

In a few minutes, Jaffe entered his room. "Need some help packing?" he asked.

"I don't have much; when do we leave?"

"Not soon enough," Jaffe quickly spit the answer. "We fly south in about two hours. The airport is just the other side of the river—I got the rental out front. We meet your wife at the gate; she wanted to do some shopping, so we have a few minutes to talk."

"I don't want to talk," Hand said. "I'm tired of talking, and I'm tired of this whole affair. The more I discuss the *event* the more pissed I get, so I'd like to just leave it all behind. Shit, we'll have to tell the whole damn story over and over for the next goddamn month. Right now I'm sick of it, and all I want is to get the hell out of this depressing city."

"Sure boss," Jaffe sarcastically said, "anything you say, but at some point we're going to have to do some comparisons, you know, C.Y.A."

"You do your own damn C.Y.A., Jaffe. My whole premise is that it happened too quickly, the more I think of it, the more confused I become, and finally, all I know is we shot, they shot, we were wounded, and they are dead. After that, I don't know shit, that's my story, it's true, and that's all I can say...to you or anyone else. We can get questioned by the ghost of fucking J. Edgar Hoover, and that's all I'm saying, because that's all I know! Period!"

"That's OK with me, Detective." Jaffe put the last few personal items in Hand's duffel bag. "I can say the exact thing, and we'll both be totally correct, but don't you wonder, I mean really *wonder*, between you, me, and the lamp post?"

"Maybe you didn't hear me? I'm tired of the whole thing, it's all I've talked about, thought, and dreamed about for days. Now, no more! Not now, and not when we get on that plane, and not until I say I want to talk to you. Shit, didn't I just tell you my story? Now drop it."

"Aye aye, Captain," Jaffe replied. "For now, I agree with you. We need to get out of here, catch some of that San Diego ocean breeze, and let our heads clear. This can wait."

"Fuck you Jaffe...wait? Wait 'til hell freezes over, I'm done. Let's go, we'll miss our damn flight if I spend all day listening to your Jewish shrink analysis of every small detail of my life. Next you'll want to know about my childhood! You're making me crazy!"

"Ever hear of PTSD?" Jaffe asked offhandedly.

"What the hell's that?" Hand replied.

"Never mind, it can wait."

"Fuck you, again."

The checkout procedure went smoothly, the only annoying

complication coming from a nurse who wanted Hand's autograph. She had a clipping from the Vancouver paper that she intended to have framed. She also informed him of the stack of inquiries for interviews from as far away as Chicago. The warm breeze that blew off the Columbia River filled Hand's lungs with cleansing relief, as he sucked deeply to remove the weeks of stagnant hospital air. The car was only fifty feet away, at the handicapped location, but Hand found himself out of breath by the time they reached the vehicle.

"To the airport, the Portland airport," Jaffe told the cabby.

Both men settled into the back seat. For Hand, it was harder to get in and be comfortable, but still, anything was a relief from the hospital. In ten minutes they were pulling up to the terminal in front of the Alaska Airlines departure area. Hand's wife came to greet them.

"Well, let's get the hero home," she said with a broad smile. The hack helped pull the luggage from the car's trunk, and with no fanfare or ado, the trio marched toward the terminal, stopping every few steps to allow Hand to catch his breath. Boarding passes were issued, and within a half hour they were in the air. Brenda contented herself with reading several women's magazines, while Jaffe mostly stared out the window. Hand took out a notepad and began writing to himself. The odd thing was, even with a return to San Diego less than two hours away, he still had a difficult time drawing the picture into focus. Things were still missing. Yes, there would be no more killings by Mark Rose, and to the entire world, that was a success. But to Detective Hand, there still existed a void, and he hoped that the writing would somehow produce the clarity needed to understand what had really happened to him, and the journey he'd taken.

At first, he thought it might well be just the quirks that accompany any homicide investigation, but quickly realized that that would not come close to satisfying the empty hunger that clawed at the pit of his stomach. There was more, not just the specifics of the investigation, for even he was now certain the final moments of Rose and Gunther's lives would always remain shrouded in mystery. There was more, and as Hand scribbled short notes to himself, he began to backtrack through the haunting phrases and murky, disconnected weave of statements from all the people who had led him to Gunther in the first place. It was there that he stopped. Suddenly he knew he was once again peering over the edge into an unknown world, and it was in this world that the answers to all that had happened would be revealed. It also made Hand feel helpless, for he knew it was a world that he could never enter... just skirt its perimeter, and try and gain a body of knowledge that would allow him rest and closure.

He penciled more thoughts, tried to figure an equation that would permit him some sense of equality with the men he'd encountered. It wasn't sameness really, but rather a policeman's need to understand what it was that caused all the death, and finally the need to get as close as he could to the inner workings of the men who nearly killed him and his partner. Men who probably *would have* killed them if it had had any relevance to what was really going on in their lives.

Hand's mind closed it, and he seemed to be alone on the plane. Trying, he thought if he somehow concentrated hard enough, focused with all his powers, that somehow, just for a moment, he might be invited into the world of these men...all of them...Rose, Doc Wood, Danny Miller, Larry Keen, the dead Marines around the country, Gunther, and his uncle. Maybe he'd be allowed to travel in their shoes, maybe he could drop in by some type of celestial magic, a cosmic opening that would let him share these men's world long enough to finally say, "I see, now I know why you're still in Viet Nam." Just as Viet Nam and the men who served there had been the answer to the current-day killings, he knew it was a foreign land that held the answers to everything. Still, it was not an objective science...two plus two would never again equal four.

His concentration was broken by the stewardess' "Buckle your seatbelt, sir, we'll be landing in about twenty minutes."

It occurred to Hand how deeply he'd gone into his own thoughts; nearly two hours had passed, and he looked at his notes and wondered if he could have somehow joined with these men if he'd had ten more minutes. But the separate reality he sought was not to be as he sat in the aircraft, yet he hoped that a resumption of the effort would bear results in another setting.

His wife turned and spoke. "Where have you been?" she asked alarmingly.

"Nowhere," he replied, "but I'll try again. It's OK, I'm still sorting, but it will be fine." He realized that he would never be able to share his quest with anyone, that he wasn't sure what he was after, or where he was going. An explanation would only alarm Brenda and cause unnecessary concern. He wondered about the Spaniard who once chased windmills. *I bet that could be me*, the thought to himself, *chasing after things that I'll never understand. Will I ever come home again? What the hell is happening?*

Lindbergh Field was a joy to embrace. The air was heavier than that of Vancouver; it didn't feel as clean, but within minutes the sub-tropical warmth began to make him realize how much he'd missed the place he lived, and he was immediately wrapped in the cocoon of security that comes with familiarity.

The San Diego police had arranged for transportation. Jaffe quickly moved toward the car first, then stopped as he realized his partner should go ahead of him. It seemed odd, they'd been together for nearly a month, and for the first time, separation between the two would be immediate. It was normal, no big deal, but odd just the same. Hand walked haltingly to the open door of the unmarked car, and before he and his wife entered, turned to Jaffe. "I'll call you tonight—we should talk before we go into the station tomorrow." Lou Jaffe got into a second car by himself.

The drive to the Hands' house took thirty minutes. Neither Dick nor Brenda spoke except to comment on how lovely it was to be home. The car's driver was a cadet, who only gave the detective an occasional glance from the rear view mirror. The sun of

San Diego County had a positive impact on the husband and wife. The gray days of Vancouver had left a pall over Dick Hand, and it was the return to his beloved San Diego that made him aware of how far down the dark road of life he'd traveled. As the car turned down the street that led to their house, he seemed to know each cactus. They pulled into the driveway, and their driver got out. The doors were opened, and the baggage emptied from the trunk. "It's a privilege to serve you, Mr. Hand." The driver extended his arm and faintly smiled. The awkward moment lasted forever, for Hand knew he had to grasp the outstretched hand and say some profound words to the young recruit. After a long ten seconds, he took the hand and said, "Thanks for your help." The man waited as if to say, "Is there more?" Hand felt fatigued, and the need to run, so he pivoted on his feet and left the driver staring at his back.

The kitchen was bright and cheerful; large windows looked into the backyard, as sun danced off the ice plants and exploding bird of paradise bushes. When the door shut, Hand remembered that he had not lifted a bag, and feeling guilty, asked his wife what he could do to help. "Nothing" she replied, "just relax, and let's see what we have to do to get things back to normal."

"I'm not sure that's in the cards," Hand snapped. "I know it's only going to be a few days before I'm standing next to dozens of internal affairs people, and the press will be asking a million questions. I just don't know what I'm gonna say. I mean, what is there to say?"

"Well, you can't say what you don't know, so it might be simpler than you think. We've been over this before, and I think if you just give it some rest, the specifics will take care of themselves. There's going to be all kinds of spin put on the story, but in the final analysis, there's only you and Lou, and after that, it's all bullshit."

Hand began to speak, not necessarily to Brenda, but just in general about ideas he had. "Every man owes a debt," he slowly drawled out. "It's a debt to yourself first, and in some ways it becomes a burden of life. But still, it must be paid. My dad paid a debt. Uncle Bill paid a debt. They served their country, served the military; they did so voluntarily: dad in Korea, Bill in Viet Nam. I did none of that, I mean, there's no draft, and there's no war, so it never occurred to me what feelings dad and Bill must have had. First debt, then pride. Both of them could have gone to school, or joined some chicken-shit National Guard outfit, but they didn't. They paid a debt, and it changed their lives. They are the men who are the backbone of this country, called to sacrifice, and doing so when other options were available. I guess I'm starting to understand, in some odd or perverted way, the world that I heard about but could have never known. It's not that I'm now one of them, it's just that I'm closer."

"I'm not sure I'm following that," Brenda said, "you're being a bit too metaphysical for me. My cousin went in the reserves back then, wanted to go to school, I guess." She took a deep breath.

"That's my point...sort of. Your cousin, all the guys who 'dodged' the draft, they did so in a bunch of ways, but in the final analysis, they ducked their obligation. Nobody was in the reserves out of any sense of *serving their country*; they all went to *avoid* com-mitment. That's why Uncle Bill and the other guys like him have such contempt for the reservists. Really, going in the reserves was just dodging the draft, just like going to Canada; it took no balls to join the reserves. At least the assholes that went to Canada had a backbone. They knew what they'd be losing, they weren't brave as such, it's just that they were leaving their own country, it must have took some balls. I mean, they weren't a real asset to America anyway, probably scum bags who the country's better off with-out. Join the reserves, get a school deferment, hell, you could even knock up your girlfriend and get out of serving your country. But the underlying reason for any of that was that you were too self-ish to serve your own country. They could legally avoid being real men. No wonder Bill hates them, I'm beginning to understand." Dick caught his breath.

Brenda spoke. "Like I said, some guys my mom knew went

in the reserves, I don't think it was that bad...I mean they still served, it's better than most of these kids today. What do these brats do now? Hell, I know kids who still live with their parents until they're thirty years old! How about that?"

"There are places these men have gone where none of us can go."

"I suppose we could book a vacation to Viet Nam in the next few years. I read that some veterans are going back, but I'm not sure what good it would do you." Brenda was running out of words, and could not catch up with Dick's line of thinking.

"It's not the *places* that make the difference, it's what the places did to the men that I'm pushing up against. Like I said, I can't really describe it, but for the first time I think I know what the men think! They've changed me, they've dragged me closer to their world, but even though I believe that, there's no way I can put it in some black-and-white police report. For now, I guess it's just rest, and to try and map out a redistricting of my world. The little boxes that were so well defined have to be moved; it's a remake of my reality, and I'm just beginning to get a grasp of that. I'm not sure where I'll land."

Hand realized he was scaring Brenda. He also knew he wasn't sure where he was going, and that was disturbing. He was wandering both mentally and emotionally, and he knew he had to bring some closure to the situation. He recognized the journey he'd begun, but was struck with fear when he knew there could be no end. No conclusion. He thought of Doc Wood: "You ever heard of PTSD?" Wood's words echoed like thunder and bounced off the walls of Hand's skull.

Brenda looked at him for several moments and did her best to mollify his uncertainty. "It will all make sense once you've had time to unwind and catch your breath. You can't expect something like this to just go away, it's traumatizing, and you just have to let things run their course. It's like a broken bone, it will heal in time."

"Easy for you to say," Hand mumbled, "but it seems so unreal, it's like it happened in another world, another lifetime. It's like Jaffe and me were characters in some coerced play; it's hard to reconcile that I'm sitting here talking with you...in our house, when just a few short weeks ago I was in a backyard ambush, fighting for my life. It's kinda like the two worlds can't exist in the same lifetime, I've really become two people."

"Well, I think it will all become clear to you with time, you've got to believe that." His wife was trying to close the discussion so that little things that normally accompanied the daily routine of living together could be accomplished. It also occurred to her that she was witnessing the transformation of her husband, and she didn't want to go the distance at this time. She was fatigued, the shootings had changed everything, and now, at blinding speed, she began to recognize that there would be no return to normalcy in their household; a new life was beginning.

"I'm gonna take a shower," Hand said. "Maybe I can wash away some of this junk. I can still smell the hospital on my skin. I hate that smell." He limped toward the bathroom and turned to his wife. "Don't worry, I'll be better—maybe I'm making things up? I don't know, but I'll be OK." Hand wasn't sure if his words sounded convincing, or if he was just recognizing the fear in Brenda's eyes. He paused and kissed her on the forehead.

Several minutes passed while Brenda stared into the wall. The phone rang, and Brenda hoped against hope that the caller would be her sister...someone not connected at all to police work.

"Hello, Hand residence."

"Hi, Mrs. Hand, this is Captain Del Vecci, central precinct, is Dick close?"

"No, I'm sorry, Captain, he's in the shower. Can I help you with something?"

"Not really, I need to talk with Dick...you know, police stuff. How's he feeling?"

"OK, I guess, it's all so incredible." Brenda hesitated; she didn't want to bring any more pressure to bear on her husband.

"Well, the whole thing's a little bizarre, but the main thing is that Dick and Jaffe are alive, and that's what I need to talk to Dick about. I need to hear first hand—I've spoken with Jaffe, and I need to coordinate a time when we all can sit down together and work out the details once more. I know we hashed this out up in Vancouver, but I want to talk with both of them again. It's important."

"Can't it wait?" Brenda asked. "I mean, Dick's been through so much, he needs some rest."

"I suppose we can wait awhile, but then I don't want Dick's memory trail going cold. I've seen a lot in my years on the force, and I tend to think that something like this can take on a life of its own. I mean, the longer you think about it, the more confusing it becomes...it's not intentional, but sometimes your mind plays tricks on you. My feeling is that the sooner we can come to grips with what happened, the sooner things will get back to normal."

"Normal," Brenda said, "well that would be nice, but I've got the feeling that normal will be a thing of the past. Dick's changed, and I'm not sure how to put this...but I don't think normal is going to be part of the equation from now on. It's hard to put your finger on, and I'm just sorting it out, maybe it's just not enough time, I don't know, but I do know Dick's different—he's so distant."

"That's why we need to talk. I've seen this in other cops over the years, and we have trained people to deal with this type of thing. But first we need Dick and Lou to come in and talk so we can begin to tie up loose ends."

Brenda hesitated. "You really think it's that easy? I mean, you just bring them in, let them talk to you and maybe a shrink or two and then...presto, all is good? Life is beautiful, and we wipe the slate clean? Like I said, Captain Del Vecci, I know Dick best, and there's something that I can't touch going on with him, and maybe it happens to anyone who nearly dies the way he did, but that's of little consequence for his family. Hell, I really don't know, and maybe I'm all wet, but we'll just have to see. Could be a little chat at the station will be all that's necessary. A get-together with other cops, you know...boys will be boys."

Captain Del Vecci waited for the sarcasm to fall before taking a patronizing page from his book. "Whatever we can do to help one of our own, we'll do, so please have Dick call me in the next hour or so."

"I'll tell him you called as soon as he's out of the shower." With that, she hung up. No thank you and no goodbye.

As she waited for her husband to come out of the bath, she wondered if it would be best to pretend the call never took place. Maybe just let sleeping dogs rest. But then her head began to flood with the combination of thoughts and equations that made any notion of delaying the inevitable impossible. This wasn't something that could be put off or in any way ducked. *Married to a cop,* she thought. *It's just part of the job, and maybe it just fades and goes away.* "Time heals all," she remembered her mother saying, but then the rush of the information overload began to seep out the recesses of her skull, and she knew that there would be no rest. For a moment she wondered if Dick would break, if there was a more serious problem that would emerge...and she knew for certain that "normal" would no longer be a part of her relationship.

"So what do you want to do?" Dick hollered from the hallway as he headed toward the bedroom.

All Brenda could think of was how to delay the coming stress and frustration that would certainly accompany her husband's involvement with Captain Del Vecci. She knew sex had to be on Dick's mind, her references to kinky activity had gotten his attention, and they had not had fun in the bedroom since the whole Vancouver fiasco had begun. Now she could get his mind on something else.

As she walked into the bedroom, her voice preceded her thoughts as she slid onto the bed and felt the comforter massage her bare thighs. "Pinky and I have had a fun relationship since you've been gone, but he's just not as much fun as when you're here," she said slowly. Pinky was the name of the vibrator that they used to augment their lovemaking. They'd been using "toys" for years, and it was something Brenda was comfortable with, especially when she learned that almost all of her female friends had at least one dildo and used it regularly. "A girl's best friend," they'd laugh among themselves; "Who needs men?" they'd joke when they went shopping. "Marital Aids" is how they were described, and they came to the house in non-descript plain packages with regularity. For Dick and Brenda, they had become a part of their sex lives, and as she spoke she felt the moisture of her juices begin to flow.

"You been using him good, huh?" Dick said as he moved to the bedside and pulled open the drawer next to them. Feelings of wicked nastiness entered Hand's head as he grabbed the vibrator with one hand and moved his fingers to his groin. "Let's see what you two have been up to over the last few weeks," he said forcefully. He turned to Brenda, unable to disguise his erect member. "Show me what you've been doing." Brenda and Hand loved to play games. Fantasy was a big part of their lovemaking. Both of them were comfortable with their human needs, and realized that variety was a big necessity in a monogamous relationship. Sexual boredom and sameness was a death factor in many relationships. That was not the case with Dick and Brenda. Over the years it had turned more raucous, and nearly anything was acceptable in their bed. Dick had wondered if the domination and control was an extension of his police work. It evolved. And finally, it was necessary for both of them to become organically satisfied.

"What do you want?" Brenda asked in her best frightened little girl voice.

"Unzip your pants and let me see your pussy," Hand said. "I want to see your wet pussy and I want to squeeze your titties while you do yourself." Hand fumbled with her shirt and, seeing her cleaved tits with the straining nipples, literally ripped at her bra, throwing it against the wall as her breasts fell free. He loved it when she sat up, letting her tits swing openly as the cherry-red nipples demanded attention. "How often has Pinky fucked you?" he asked, as he gently pushed and flicked her swollen titties.

"A lot," Brenda said, "I've been a bad girl, but what I've really wanted was to do myself in front of you again. Watch me fuck myself...slap them harder...now." She leaned slightly forward as her tits moved rhythmically, inviting attention. At first, Hand just squeezed and gauged her reaction. He knew the game, it wasn't really pain, but close to it, for he'd found out years ago that Brenda loved the idea of mild force, and as a cop he'd handcuffed his wife more than once. He reached out and grabbed both nipples, twisting them together until he heard Brenda, "...ouch, ouch, oh God that hurts, now slap them...slap them good!"

"What will you do for me if I do?" Hand demanded.

"I'll spread my legs and put Pinky way in my pussy, I'll let you watch, I'll be real bad."

"Pull your pants off," Hand said.

Brenda lifted her ass slightly and removed her shorts. "Leave your panties on," he said. With that, he lowered himself to her thigh and positioned his face close to her crotch.

"Hold perfectly still," Hand demanded. "If you move one more time, I'll stop licking, and take Pinky away from you." Hand knew his request would be impossible; he'd never known a woman who could resist good cunnilingus, and Brenda was certainly no exception. It was part of their game, and soon he covered her clitoris with his mouth and sucked viciously. It was domination and pleasure. Brenda squirmed and gyrated under Hand's mouth. He abruptly stopped and pulled away from her.

"I can't help it," she cried, "please do what you want, I'll try and be better, but my pussy wants you and Pinky both."

All part of the game, he thought to himself—they'd done this hundreds of times. As Brenda stood and bent over, grabbing the foot board, she asked meekly, "you're going to spank me, huh....well I deserve it, I just couldn't be still." Hand's injured leg throbbed, but the excitement of seeing his wife's ass was too overwhelming. He pulled her panties down to her thigh. Her breasts hung perpendicular and swayed in the most provocative manner. Hand began with a swift short smack. Brenda's flesh jiggled from the impact. The noise excited them both, and within seconds Brenda was raising her ass higher, her cheeks red with pleasure.

"Hurt me good, Officer Hand!" She knew what to do next. With one hand she grabbed the dildo and inserted it into her waiting vagina. Hand slowed the gentle spanking and watched as his wife performed their ritualistic sex and voyeurism. He pushed his penis into her waiting lips and began to pump wildly. It seemed like forever since they'd had sex, and Hand knew he wouldn't last long. He grabbed her and pushed her flat onto her back on the bed. . He took long strokes, and in less than a minute let loose what seemed like gallons of fluid in Brenda's throat. She moaned as she swallowed, and Hand began to go limp.

After several minutes, Hand rolled to his side. His wife lay with her panties still on and the vibrator alongside her open thighs. "Jesus," Hand said, "I'd forgotten how fun it is to be this nasty with you."

"We're just starting, Sweets," Brenda replied, "there's plenty more where that came from...God I'm getting kinky in my old age. I've been waiting to tell you all these fantasies...you know, play act. I'm so glad you're home, there's lots to make up for."

"I can hardly wait," Hand said. "Is four o'clock too soon?" He laughed, and then casually noted, "I suppose I better call the office. Del Vecci is likely to have a cow if I don't get down there and kiss his ass soon."

"He already called," Brenda said, "I just wanted to welcome you home before you had to get back to work."

"What a welcome," Hand grinned. He reached and twisted her nipple hard. "Better get out of here or I'll lose my job to a nasty wife and Pinky."

"His number's on the counter in the kitchen; I think he's on a cell phone. See if you can delay your meeting, we've got to spend some time together...I mean, we're husband and wife, you'd think that Del Vecci thinks he owns you."

"Well, the SDPD like to take care of their own, but you'd think if he knew what I had waiting here, he'd give me some time alone. Maybe a few days." Hand sighed.

"I doubt that anything we have to attend to has ever crossed his mind. Besides, there's a huge hole that the police need to fill, and I bet they want another piece of you two long before the reporters arrive." Brenda waited, and Hand thought of his next move.

"There's really not much to say," he droned. "I'll fill out a bunch of other reports...hell I should just xerox the ones I did in Vancouver, that should do!"

"No, it won't," Brenda replied. "Maybe you should phone Jaffe first...you know, coordinate your thinking?"

"Why?" Dick asked. "There's nothing to coordinate. I mean, what happened is history, so it's not like we need a lead-in story line. Give me the phone." For the first time, he noticed his leg pulsing. As he painfully pulled on his underpants and trousers, he knew he was correct...there was nothing much to say, his mind began to spin and he saw the huge muzzle flash of the .45 go whipping past his forehead. He knew, simultaneously, that there was *much* he *could* say, but the disturbing distance that he was traveling was best kept to himself. He hoped he had the poise to hide his personalized terror.

"Lou, it's Dick. Del Vecci just called, so I thought I'd ring you up and see what the hell we should do. I feel like a sheep being led into the slaughterhouse, but we gotta face the music sometime, and I wondered what you think about all this shit."

"Nothing to think," Jaffe replied, "there's just gonna be a bunch of paperwork and about a million forms. I don't think it's gonna be a big deal, I mean, what's to say? And hell, we can't stay home forever. Really, I want to get all the crap behind us and get back to work. And who's kidding who, Del Vecci tore up Gunther's 'goodbye' note, and he thinks he's got it all figured. We went through all this in Vancouver, so I think this is just a dog and pony show for all the brass here in San Diego. Just remember, we *never* heard of or saw any type letter from Gunther or anyone else. We'll get beyond this...no problem. Keeping busy is the best remedy; we can't sit around all our lives and think about crap we can't change, so call him up and let's get rolling. You want me to do it?"

"Nah, I'll call him," Hand rebuffed, "he'll probably give me some cushy office job while this hole in my leg mends, but I want to make sure that he doesn't reassign you to a different partner on a permanent basis. We gotta stick together, I don't want any *divide and conquer* crap going on down at headquarters."

"There's nothing to divide or conquer...nothing to really discuss. We were there...*you're* the one who said it, we were there, it happened in a few seconds, and it's over, so what else is there to say?" Jaffe waited until he knew there would be no further discussion.

"OK, I'll give him a call and make a time to get the show on the road. Any time better for you?"

"Nope, I'm just here waiting around, but let's do it during the day, I think we'll both want a drink or six when this is over, so don't schedule it for evening...we'd probably get stuck there for half the night."

Jaffe waited, and after a few seconds' pause, Hand replied. "I'll call you back in a few minutes. Brenda said he's on his cell phone, so it won't be hard to find him. He'll want to give us a bunch of advice on handling the media, but I think it's all crap...after all, what's to say?"

With that, Hand hung up the phone and stared at his surroundings. At once it seemed eerily quiet, and for the moment his wife floated into a different part of the house. He was alone, or it certainly felt that way. It was as if he'd departed to another place that was still in the house but really wasn't *there*. He was a picture out of focus, and time hung suspended as he felt himself go into a trance of sorts that left him relaxed, yet unable to move. A tingle started at his neck and spread down his back. Any sense of pain or worry left his body. *This must be like a Hindu mantra*, he thought to himself. *I'm just floating and I'm here...but I'm not really part of this world. It's not bad, really, just weird, and I don't want it to stop. Just let me lift off, just kinda stay suspended from the world I knew, just float outside the bubble and peer back on life from my new position.* Then he wondered if this is what death must be. Serenity, calm and peaceful, a world without questions. Composure. He hoped it would never end, for in this world there were no guns, no muzzle blasts, no screams, no blood, no exit wounds, and no body parts.

"Dick what are you doing?" his wife's voice called from a distant place that echoed through a fog.

He looked at Brenda for a long moment. Her features began to take shape, and it was only when he'd reemerged from his lapse into the netherworld that he could see the look of concern on her face.

"Where have you been?" Brenda jokingly said. The wrinkles on her brow told him there was more to her question than he wanted to answer.

"I just drifted off, that's all. Don't worry, it's no big deal; I guess it's just good to be home." He wondered if his explanation sounded as shallow as he felt saying the words. Somehow he knew different things were happening in his life, things he could not control, things that were sweeping him along...things that he could not help but to carry, things that would be a load to bear, things that would keep him up at night. Just short glimpses now, but the journey to places in his mind and consciousness that didn't exist before. Places that were never supposed to be discovered. Doors that were not designed to be opened, feelings that he'd never known before his trip to Vancouver. At first he dismissed the surprise attacks as something that would pass, just effects of the ambush from the garden. It would heal, like any wound. But he was now coming to the dread reality that the world he'd entered was a trap that had no exit. The effects, he now began to realize, were post-traumatic effects, and the benign words of Doc Wood thudded off his brain. Like Alice falling into the rabbit hole, Hand had inadvertently opened his own ambush, one he couldn't control and whose visits were determined by circumstances that he couldn't define or explain.

"Ever heard of PTSD?"...he felt the rush of Doc Woods' voice cover his soul. And then, "Gunther's not finished with you."

"Captain, this is Dick Hand, sorry for the delay, but there's so much I didn't expect. I mean this has been quite the trip, but I'm ready to get together most any time. So is Jaffe, but we think earlier is better than late in the day, how's that sound?" Hand realized he was struggling to sound nonchalant, almost flippant, and was happy that there was a telephone between him and John Del Vecci.

"Dick, Jesus how are you?" Del Vecci's tone went personal before anything else could be said. "God it's good to hear your voice, I called a couple of times, did Brenda tell you? I know it hasn't been that long since Vancouver, but still, I was worried."

"Yeah, she did, and like I said, I had a few immediate needs to attend to, I've been away for longer than I thought, and with Brenda coming up to the Vancouver hospital, it left the house in a mess. All that crap can wait, so I just want to say it's good to be in San Diego, and I'd like somehow to get back to work soon—I think too much idle time will not be good for me. So when do you want to meet? I'll let Jaffe know and we'll get together and figure out all the world's problems!"

"Tomorrow's fine with me, as early as you want, but are you sure you're feeling up to it?"

"Yeah, sure," Hand replied, "how long can this take? I'm sure you've read all the reports a million times since you were in Vancouver, so there's really not much to add. We can fill in a few blanks I guess, but it shouldn't take long. After all, there are some *things* that are better left out of the discussion. Right? So how about ten o'clock...in your office?"

"Ten's fine with me, but be prepared—in a case like this, it's never as simple as you would like. Two men are dead, two officers wounded, Vancouver police are pissed off, the media wants to pick apart the whole affair, the city shrink wants to analyze both of you, and the chief can't make up his mind if he wants to give you awards or hang your ass. So don't think this is going to be a walk in the park. But we gotta start somewhere, so make it ten in the morning, and plan to stay awhile. And you're right, there are some things that will never be spoken, it's just better that way."

Hand phoned Jaffe, but left out the details. Somehow he knew he'd have to save his strength for morning, and any preparing with Jaffe could be done in the car on the way in. Besides, talking about how to coordinate their morning meeting would just lead to more conjecture and speculation. Hand knew that Lou Jaffe was made more nervous by the posturing, and he didn't want to open a can of worms over the phone. Jaffe would want to talk incessantly, and all the talk in the world would accomplish nothing. For now he wanted rest, and he wanted time to try and get a grip on the events that were sliding into his brain, and to control the thoughts that now appeared from nowhere and randomly took his mind to places it had never been.

Morning arrived, but Hand was far from refreshed. He'd wanted sleep, and it came in fitful intervals that left him more concerned for his sanity than he cared to consider. A gradual uneasiness entered his thoughts...he was beginning to fear sleep. It was something that he'd pushed aside and told himself it was a passing condition that would abate with time. Now he wasn't so sure. He feared sleep because with sleep came the possibility of hallucinations, nightmares really, and sleep left him no control over the dreams. They came, voices from unseen, dark places beckoned him down paths where explosions rocked him awake, leaving him panting and bathed in sweat. *It will get better*, he thought, but he was increasingly terrified that he'd again be visited by Tim Gunther... the man who haunted his nights, moving slowly like oil on water, casting a sideways glance at Hand, a leering smile seeming to say, "Welcome to my world."

Brenda slept late, and for that Hand was thankful. The morning was nothing short of spectacular, and the bright sun had a positive effect on Hand's thinking. He didn't fix any coffee, knowing the aroma would wake his wife. Instead he sat on the front porch and tried to gather his recollections. He did his best to insulate himself from going places he didn't want to go. *Stay focused,* he repeated to no one, *keep it short and simple: we were there, shots were fired, people died, and...I guess we killed them.* Problem was, in his heart he knew the story was wrong. He knew Doc Wood was right. From the bushes off to the side of the house, Hand thought he saw movement. Just a shadow maybe. Wind and faint footsteps. He stood up and took several steps. The stiffness of the wound to his thigh restricted his movement and slowed him down. His body tingled, hair rose on his back as he stared into nothing but felt the certainty of unseen company and felt the grip of an unseen hand. The detective slowly walked toward the backyard of his home. Instinctively, he began to crouch, and felt the tremble of fear that swept his psyche when he recalled he was without his weapon. *This is stupid,* he thought, *Christ, I'm in my own yard, what the hell am I doing out here, crawling around like an Indian?*

Nothing. There was nothing in Hand's backyard, just the gentle breeze that rocked the lush vegetation. He turned and retraced his footsteps, *I must be going nuts,* he said to no one. Then he thought about what a neighbor might think if he was passing by for a morning walk.

"Where were you?" Brenda asked with a look of concern. She gathered her bathrobe, and asked him if he wanted coffee.

"Just walking in the yard, you know, it takes some doing to loosen up. The wounds hurt, and all at once I'm feeling a hundred years old." He hesitated for a moment. "Thanks for asking."

Hand walked past Brenda and faintly said, "I'm not hungry, I'll just shower and get this damn day over with. Jaffe's picking me up a little before ten, right?"

"That's what you said last night, so I guess nothing's changed—at least nothing I know of—but then who am I to be informed?" They both looked at each other, and as their eyes locked, they both grasped how much *everything* had changed. Dick went in the house to use the toilet. Brenda looked at him and wanted to speak, but knew the time was wrong and that her thoughts might do more harm than good on a morning like this. He closed the bathroom door behind himself, and for the first time in his memory, he set the lock.

The hot water ran as the room steamed up. Dick Hand stared into the mirror until his reflection became blurred and only then did he remember why he was in the room. He turned the water to cold as he let the pulsing moisture hit his flesh.

"Feeling better? You must have fallen back to sleep in there." Brenda offered some lightness to the morning. She was now seriously wondering what type of problems her husband was developing. Brenda didn't want to be the first one to bring up the idea of visiting a counselor or shrink. She feared Dick's reaction...he'd insist nothing was wrong, and that psychologists were for weaklings.

"I am better, thanks," Dick said. "I think I'm making more of this than need be." He paused, "there's more to life, and I've just got to realize that this is a pretty unusual time, and it'll get better." For a moment, Hand almost believed himself, and as if to reassure Brenda, he reached up under her robe and squeezed the cheek of her buttocks.

"I've got something in mind to make you better in a heartbeat," Brenda said mischievously, "and honey is it gonna be *good*. I've been lonely too long, and I'm so ready to be nasty...oh shit, I wish Jaffe wasn't coming, because I'm the one who wants to do the physical interrogation. I mean, I think I know how to get some answers…and fast!" She winked and opened the front of her robe, exposing her swinging breasts.

"The wait will make it better," Hand smiled, "we'll see what tonight brings, huh?"

"This debriefing with old Captain *What's-his-nuts* better be the shortest in history…pinky might just get worn out before you get back!"

They both heard the car enter the driveway, and knew it could only be Jaffe. "Put it on hold and keep it wet and juicy for me." Hand raised her gown and gave her a quick slap across the butt.

"Oh God, talk about wet, I'm already starting to ooze." The doorbell rang.

"Hey troop," Jaffe intoned, "how's the man with all the holes?"

"Gettin' stronger every day," Hand replied. "Got to get this shit out of the way, I mean, Del Vecci sounds like a menopausal woman—I can't believe he calls here about every hour, making sure I don't run away or some such crap."

Jaffe walked past Hand and hugged Brenda. "You takin' care of this guy?" he laughed, as their bodies collided.

"I'm trying to be all things to all people," Brenda responded, "but the sooner we get all the formalities behind us, the sooner we can start to put the house back together…if you know what I mean."

"This will be over soon," Jaffe said to both Brenda and Dick. "We just stay focused and give them what they want to hear, and bingo…you blink twice and it will be Christmas. Don't sweat the small stuff, this is just routine."

"Sure, right," Hand muttered sarcastically, "let's get the hell out of here and get this crap over with, I already want a double bourbon." He gave Brenda a kiss and limped bravely toward the door. "Believe me, I'll be back as soon as I can fly. I wish that damn Del Vecci didn't sound so mysterious about the whole thing, you'd think he'd be more sympathetic, he makes it sound like the whole department wants to ream our ass...I mean, all we did was nearly get killed!"

"OK cowboy, we'll sort it out later, let's go." Jaffe nodded toward the door, and signaled that it was time to leave. With that, the two officers walked into the bright sun and drove to their appointment with the captain and with the unspoken monster that waited just beneath the surface.

Hand buckled his seatbelt and sat looking straight ahead. He felt his thoughts slipping and rolled down the window. Sometimes he found himself just floating from one place to another, lifted by unseen forces that pushed him into alleyways of darkness where he didn't want to go...and from where there was no escape. It was becoming more frequent, and Hand was privately beginning to worry for his own future and sanity. As his wife had slept, he'd accessed web sites with information about PTSD. The indications of what to be aware of and what to look out for were scary to Hand. There was a problem, and it was growing. He knew it, but still hung to the hope that it would fade, that normalcy would return and he'd be the person he was before he met Tim Gunther and Mark Rose. He was human, he was different than his demons. He told himself he had nothing to fear, he was strong—stronger than this PTSD crap. It was reserved for Viet Nam veterans, not Dick Hand. As the days passed, he knew that wasn't going to happen any time soon and the uncertainty of where he'd be taken haunted his moves. Dick Hand was a fighter, and at this point, resignation to his fate was not an option.

"Cat got your tongue?" Jaffe smoothly prodded. The mere reference to a tongue made Hand's head snap back.

"More than my tongue, I think. Might have my whole damn head," Dick replied with a flick of the wrist. He had to remind himself of who Jaffe was...he felt adversarial and distant. It was a question of control, and he knew it wasn't going to be an easy task to keep his balance through the upcoming meeting.

The rest of the half-hour journey was covered with small talk, and Hand found a sense of relief and security as they pulled into the parking lot of the police station. Just the comfort of being in the company of fellow officers gave him a sense of firm resolve as they entered the closeted world of the uniformed police building.

"I don't want to talk to anyone," Hand said.

"What do you mean? We're here to talk to Del Vecci for Christ's sake, how do you arrive at the notion of *not talking*?"

"I mean, I don't want to talk to any of the men, you know, no back slapping and all that shit. I just don't feel like a warm-up, I just want to see Del Vecci and get the hell out."

"Jesus, you just said it was refreshing to be back with all these cops, now you want to run for cover! What gives with you anyway, you're making less and less sense. What do you think we should do, wear disguises, maybe go in with bags over our heads, or an old Ronald Reagan mask?" Lou Jaffe realized he had overstated his case, and for an instant made a mental note to try and find out what *really* was going on in his partner's head. But now wasn't the time, now they needed all their strength, and whatever was between them could wait.

They walked unnoticed through the underground parking garage, and took the elevator to the fourth floor. Captain Del Vecci's door was open, but there was nobody in the room. A few people walked past in the hallway and cast sideways glances at the two as they stood uncomfortably in the middle of the office, slowly turning to steady themselves with the setting. At once, John Del Vecci entered the office, looking as normal as anybody on the street. There was nothing that stood out about Captain Del Vecci. Maybe it was the administrative side of him; it was well known that the captain had very little street time and was more of a bureaucrat than a cop.

"Get the door fellas, and get off your feet. Christ, it's good to see the two of you in the flesh." John Del Vecci moved forward with his hand extended, "You guys aren't disappointed that there's not a room full of people, are you?"

The following minutes were filled with small talk and the normal chat about family and comforts. After the perfunctory and sometimes inane jabber, the captain leaned back in his chair and opened a file folder that was in the center of his desk. "I don't want to spend any more time than necessary," Del Vecci said, "but we have to get what happened straight from your mouth. You know we've heard just about every wild tale that you can imagine, accounts from about fifty different people and a hundred different newspapers. All I want to do is to get the story right the first time, and to caution you to avoid too much talk with the press. You know you'll have to talk to some other people here too...shrinks, and all sorts of 'do-gooders.' I know it will be impossible to avoid once the bastards know you're back in town, but try and keep it to a minimum. I'd try and keep you out of the entire loop, but most of this is out of my league, it has to run its course, and it will be uncomfortable. The more information these guys get, the more they twist the story, and pretty soon you're back to square one... that is, a whole bunch of disconnected crap that makes everybody look bad. So a word to the wise, keep your lips shut and you'll be safer. We still understand each other, right? Keep it simple and to the point...and *some* things never happened."

"No problem, John," Hand quipped, "here's the story. We walked in, they shot, we shot back, they died, we didn't. How's that for interesting reading?"

"For the media, I hope it passes, that would be nice, but for now, we'll need to be a bit more specific. I don't need to go over the whole story, most of it's pretty clear, it's just those ten or fifteen seconds that we need to get straight...then we're out of the woods."

Dick Hand thought to himself...*just those few seconds, wouldn't that be nice? Just like a simple kids' puzzle—put together the pieces and your life is whole again. Presto, I'm normal.* It was obvious to Hand that he'd never be able to describe to Del Vecci how he felt, or where he'd been. The distance between him and most of the rest

of the world had become too great, and for now he'd have to con-
centrate on bullshitting his way through this interview.

Dick glanced at Jaffe, as if to say, "you go first." There was an
awkward silence, and to break the impasse Del Vecci said, "Do
you think you really killed them? I mean, are you confident the
exchange of fire was that clean and clear? You shot, they shot, and
when all was over, they were dead, and you two were hauled to the
hospital?"

"That's all I know, Captain," Dick replied in barely concealed
hostile tones. Hand had to control his emotions, for if he'd blurted
out what he really felt...that Del Vecci probably couldn't write a
traffic ticket, and had no right to question him or his partner, he
might blow the whole interview. "It happened so fast, really, it's
nothing like the simulation crap we go through. I guess the training's better than nothing, but all the same, where the shit hits the
fan, it's a whole different story."

Hand wondered if the captain could read his mind. He wondered if Del Vecci knew what he knew. Hand remembered the
rounds going over his head, and wondering why Gunther and Rose
had stopped the slaughter. Were they injured too badly? Was the
return fire by the two cops that effective and accurate? In his heart
of hearts he knew, but nobody was in a position to speculate, so
why bring up the possibility? They'd walked into an ambush like
pigs to the butcher, but for some reason they were spared. There
was no rationalizing it, and to open that can of worms would help
nothing, so he shrugged his shoulders and concluded, "Fastest few
seconds of my life, I'll play it over in my head forever, but that's
all I know. We shot, they shot. I don't know why, Rose was coming
to kill Gunther, and they end up trying to kill us. Go figure, hell
if I know."

"The Vancouver coroner says both those guys were shot by
your guns, but both died from a .45 round. Neither of you used a
.45, you both carry 9mm, so what do you make of that?" Another
long moment ensued.

"Can't explain any of that, sir," Jaffe injected his opinion, "we weren't counting rounds, there were no time-outs."

Both men looked at each other. Hand and Jaffe knew that the subject of Gunther's letter was taboo, and therefore this whole discussion was a moot exercise. So, this interview must be for internal purposes only. Hell, maybe it was being taped?

Hand wanted to say what he felt. Both Rose and Gunther had made up their minds to commit suicide that night, but why was it necessary to include him and Jaffe in their twisted scheme? Still, he didn't want to bring that up, it would just prolong the agony of the interview, and would not get them any closer to answers. Hand knew they were not dealing in absolutes; there was no two-plus-two equation that would lead them out of the woods. Why would people he didn't even know want to kill him? Or did they want him dead? His head spun, and he knew he'd have to never divulge his true thinking. What good would it do?

"Captain, we know the probable motive for their actions, and," Hand hesitated and looked toward the door to insure that it remained closed, "and so, is this line of questioning a sort of rehearsal or drill? I mean given the *thing* we want to omit, isn't it better to stick to the 'we shot, they shot' script? We all know that the coroner will eventually leak information to the press or someone else who will ask the obvious questions. But Lou and I had no idea of what these two were up to...hell, we just walked into the fray. And so, there will never be an 'answer,' it's not that easy. Again, this ain't objective logic...two plus two will forever equal six. Too many unknowns."

The talk went on for over an hour, with no questions being solved, and as Hand wasn't about to open up completely, when the discussion was over they didn't know any more than when they'd begun. That was as he had hoped, because his world was now so much different than that of his peers, it was just easier to say, "they shot, we shot."

"Well Dick, you're on casual duty for now, until you and the doctor think you're strong enough to join Lou in the field. Doc says it will probably be the better part of three months. We want to be careful; I mean, you could easily re-injure the leg if you pushed it too hard, too fast. In the meantime, take the rest of the week off and relax, and if you need anything, you let me know. Next week we'll find you a nice office job...something you're sure to hate, but what the hell, you'll see how the other half lives. This is an odd deal, but thankfully it took place in Vancouver and not here, the press would never let go of it. Anyway, I've got some clippings from the Vancouver paper, thought you'd like to keep them...maybe a scrapbook or something." He handed Dick and Lou identical bits of articles from the Vancouver *Columbian*.

"Thanks, I guess," Hand said, "but, for now, a scrapbook seems like the last thing I want. I'd rather forget the whole damn thing...maybe in time..." He trailed off, not wanting to alert the captain to the real fear that was building in his bones.

"Oh, Dick, one more thing, I almost forgot. You got this package from Vancouver; it says 'personal' on it, so it's probably from some secret admirer." John Del Vecci forced a laugh. "Kinda odd though, no return address, and it's postmarked a couple of days before the shootout. How would someone know you were about to be 'famous' *before* the bullets started to fly? It's been sitting here for quite a while, so I thought I'd pass it on." He gave the brown, wrapped box to Hand and hesitated, as if he expected Dick to open it in front of him and Jaffe.

"I'll look at it later," Dick said. "Right now I want a drink, and to try and think of something other than this shit. Thanks for your help, Captain."

With that, the two turned and left.

"Listen guys," Del Vecci yelled after them, "be prepared for more people asking this same line of questioning. I'm sure none of us has heard the last of this crap, so keep your powder dry."

They drove north, out of the city, while making small talk. Both the men danced around the obvious subject that dominated their lives. As they moved inland from Del Mar, Dick pointed to a comfortable-looking Mexican restaurant and bar. "Let's stop there for a drink. I remember they have a real nice patio—I loved the tile the last time Brenda and I were here."

Jaffe pulled into the lot and turned off the engine. "You gonna open your mystery present? Let's see what you got, just like Christmas in July."

Dick shoved the package under the seat. "Nah, I'll wait until later, I don't need any more bullshit in my life right now. Hell, it's probably some assorted directions for how to handle emotional stress, or some group of do-gooders who want me to write a book. Don't need it. For now I need a drink and a cool breeze."

"Well," Jaffe pulled back, "the do-gooders you're talking about must be clairvoyant, I mean, how did they send you a package before the event?"

The outdoor seating area was just as Dick remembered, colorful and relaxing. Two bourbons were ordered and the waitress helped the limping Dick Hand into his chair.

"Well, that crap with Del Vecci went much better that I thought it would," Jaffe offered. "Almost smooth," he further intoned. "I was wondering when the other shoe was going to drop, but the captain seemed almost nice...no, he was nice, I guess we're making too much out of this. I just hope upcoming talks with other creeps go as well. I wonder when we'll have to see the chief? God, what a thought."

"Cut the crap Lou," Dick stopped his partner, "Del Vecci was nice because he had no choice. I hope you know we're involved up to our ass in a cover-up, and the captain is in too deep to let the truth out. This has nothing to do with 'nice,' it's all a question of protection, and the best we can do is to C.Y.A. Keep your mouth shut, and we're OK."

Lou Jaffe shook his bowed head. "I hope we're not creating a monster; if anyone ever hears of that letter, I think we'd be done for. Seems clear to me that those two had this planned. But for what reason?"

Hand listened as the drinks came, and ordered two more before the first sip was taken. He heard Jaffe's words, but his mind wandered, and he began to feel himself slip into the world of fantasy and dilution. He wanted to tell Jaffe that he'd stumbled upon the reason that worked for him, but relating that thought was as impossible as it was scary. Across the patio, in the tall tropical plants of the terrace, Hand thought he saw movement. Just a faint rustle of the broad-leaf palms, and he instinctively began to look for cover and concealment.

"Hey, you listening?" Jaffe's voice boomed.

"Sorry." Hand jolted. "I just drifted off, you know, just still trying to shake this thing. But, listen, you're right, it was an easier meeting than I expected it would be, but believe me, we haven't heard the last of this. We'll be having to tell this story for months, and I don't know about you, but for me, I don't want to think of that burden...I just want to forget it. How to be normal again... that's what gets to me. I don't know, but this situation has me worried, I mean I'm *seeing* things—things I shouldn't be seeing—and I just want it to go away."

It wasn't the first time Jaffe frowned as he listened to his disturbed partner. As he nursed his drink, and Hand guzzled his, Lou began to realize that there was something profoundly different between the way Hand had been affected by the shooting, and the way they both felt. Sure, he was also traumatized, but he wasn't consumed by the event. He felt certain that it would go away, and at some point just be another story about police work. Maybe one of folklore, but still one that simply became part of the police picture. And who was kidding who; something like this could easily lead to early promotions, they were both big names in the department. As he stared at Hand, he wondered how badly he was really hurt. Yes, Hand had sustained the more serious injuries, but Jaffe was beginning to realize that Hand's problems were more than the bullet injuries As his partner and friend, he felt awkward asking too many prying questions, but at the same time, didn't want to leave him alone. He was there, and that made him the best sounding board for the mental problems he now knew Dick was experiencing. Still, he was no shrink, and he waited for the second bourbon to be finished before he asked the next question.

"You really mean that, don't you?" Jaffe asked.

"Yeah, Lou, I do, and to tell you the truth, it has me scared shitless. I mean I don't want to make a big deal of it, sound like some pussy, but hell, things aren't right, I feel like a pachinko ball on a pinball machine, I just can't get out of the game. I keep getting beat from side to side, I can't get the shit out of my head. I don't want to frighten Brenda or the captain...or for that matter you...but I gotta tell you, I'm not sure what all this means except that I feel like I'm in a time warp that has a maniacal grip...and I'm scared. Hell, if I told the captain my *real* dreams, he'd have me under psychiatric study...shit, who knows, I could lose my job!" Hand took a breath and realized how fast he'd been talking, and how Jaffe's face had a concerned look of disbelief. The waitress stood before them, and Hand figured she'd been waiting there for several minutes.

"Uh...uh, would you like another?" she said, forcing a smile.

Dick looked at Lou, who nodded, and he said, "Yes, thank you, we'll have two more."

"Maybe you *should* get some help," Lou said. "I mean there's no script for what we went through, and everybody takes it differently." For a moment Jaffe felt guilty for lecturing Dick; after all, Hand was the ranking officer, and theoretically he was in charge, so the careful words Jaffe chose felt uncomfortable. He also knew that whatever Dick Hand was experiencing was not a problem that he shared. He knew intuitively that he'd have no problem carrying on a normal life.

"I think I'll go see my uncle," Hand said out of the blue. "Uncle Bill, you met him a couple of times, you know, the guy who lives up in Laguna, he's nutty as a pet rock, but I think I'd feel better talking to him, I think he might have a better idea of what kinda mental crap I've got to handle. I really don't know where else to go, I mean, I can't cry on your shoulder forever, and it would scare Brenda half to death, Del Vecci would probably have me committed, and the press would have a field day writing about some cop's problem coping. Yeah, I'll go see my crazy uncle...hell, I never thought we'd have much in common, always thought he was nuts, and a bit of a storyteller, but I think I'm beginning to see a glimpse of his world."

"Well, don't you think you should let Brenda know what you're up too?" Jaffe made it clear that he didn't approve of the spontaneous decisions that Hand was making.

"Lou, this is so odd, so out of control, you have to trust me on this one. Somehow, I feel that a time with my weird uncle is all I have to make any sense of my situation."

Jaffe quietly grunted a "yes" as he tried to fathom what he'd just heard from his partner. He hoped he was concealing the shock of his emotions, and searched for upbeat words to end the terrifying discussion they'd just had. He couldn't ingest the depths of the confusion that he'd witnessed, and he fumbled for something profound to say. "Maybe it's that 'post-traumatic' stuff old Doc Wood talked about? You know, that Navy guy with one leg? Hell, I forget what he meant, but he said a bunch of guys had it, maybe there's some sort of treatment, or you can talk to someone. Hey, San Diego has a whole group of shrinks on retainer, and I always thought it was a waste of money, but hell, maybe you should go see one, they might give you some sort of medicine. For sure, you can't let this get out of hand, I mean if it's that stress trauma, or whatever they call it, there's got to be some kind of pill or something you can take to get over it."

"I'll talk to my uncle," Dick said, suddenly feeling helpless and vulnerable. Thinking of his Uncle Bill made him feel almost childish, but he knew he had no choice but to try and find a remedy for the whiplash ambushes that were now controlling his life.

Jaffe dropped him off in front of his house. "I'll be at the office tomorrow," he said. "Call me if you need anything, and take it easy—don't let this shit beat you up. It'll be OK, believe me." Jaffe knew his words were just empty comments, but he didn't know what else to say. He felt stupid, for he couldn't believe how hollow his voice sounded. He also felt guilty. He couldn't figure out how the two of them had experienced the same thing, and yet he was feeling none of the fear and trepidation of his partner. Yes, Hand had sustained the worse wounds, but still, they both were *there*, and had felt the terror mutually. But Lou really knew that he was normal. He also knew Dick was totally different...he was slipping somewhere that Lou couldn't travel.

"Where's that present I got from Vancouver?" Hand asked.

"Shit, I almost forgot, your secret admirer sent you this gift, and we almost left it under the seat. Must be getting old." Jaffe handed Dick the brown package and hesitated, as if to say, "open it."

"I'll be in touch," Dick said, "and keep cool, there's going to be a lot more questions; I'm not sure we'll ever live this down. Keep it simple: they shot, we shot—I'm not sure I could handle any more stress, if *certain* things got out."

As Hand walked up his driveway, he stared at the odd unidentified parcel in his hand. He really had no idea what to expect, but he somehow felt that he should throw it in the trash—yet like an anxious child, he knew he'd want to see the contents. *Can't be much*, he thought to himself; it was probably some crackpot with a proposal for a huge book deal, or some phony speaking proposition. But how?—the postmark was *before* the shooting. Maybe the stamp was dated wrong, some postal worker who forgot to change the date. The house was empty, and he found a note from Brenda saying she'd be home around five o'clock. That gave him two hours to kill. He sat on the edge of their bed and eyed the little brown package. "This is stupid," he said to no one, and he tore into the wrapping and exposed a cardboard box. Pulling back the lid, he saw a carefully folded white paper that he knew instinctively could not account for the weight of the box. Hand removed the paper, waited half a second, and screamed in horror, as he threw the box to the wall, and jumped off the bed.

Terror gripped the fiber of his being as the walls closed in and he sweated and panted like a trapped animal in a locked car. He paced and fretted as he considered his next move, glancing at the box almost as if it were an adversary, talking to himself, then finding he was growling like a dog ready to attack. Approaching the package, he nimbly took out the paper, holding it like a soiled diaper at arms length, turning it against the light of the bedroom window as he held it between his thumb and index finger. Hand-writing covered the inside of the paper, and after Hand had determined there was no danger in opening the letter, he sat on the edge of his bed and carefully unfolded the missive.

In very clear, concise lettering, the contents of the note poured over Hand in a way that seemed natural, yet unfair.

> *Dear Detective Hand,*
>
> *I sent you this little "gift" anticipating that I wouldn't be here to deliver it in person. Things happen...right? Anyway, I don't dislike you personally, otherwise you'd be dead. For me, I just knew it was time to leave, and really it was easy. With or without Rose, it was time to go, and I felt no hesitation. There is no explaining the life I've led after Viet Nam, every day was a joke. Nothing approached a single day I spent in the bush, and really there's no way to convey any of that. My world is so far removed from yours, there is nothing that can be done or said to make any sense of it. In a way, it terrorizes me, but in an odd way it's what I really knew, and it was the best time of my life. Now I miss it more than ever...it's just there's nothing that gives me the thrill, and to go through life*

knowing your best asset is to stalk the jungle and kill...and to also know you'll never be able to do it again, makes for an odd existence.

My life is now over, I hope I'm with friends...warriors from centuries gone by...I don't know. I do know that I won't be having any need for these cute little mementos of the bush... and I don't want them falling into the hands of some dumbass shrink to analyze me in death...so they're yours. Maybe they will allow you to see me a little more clearly, I don't know, but my choice was easy, and it's now up to you to see if the parts change your life.

Tim Gunther

The quiet of the room closed in on him. Dead silence. It was midday and it seemed dark. Yet he somehow knew that he was being ushered into a strange new realm...a kingdom of oddities that made him sense a profound difference with his current surroundings.

Hand slowly put down the letter and walked to the box. The fear he first felt was leaving his psyche, being replaced with the feeling of being transported through one dimension to another. At the same time, a strange wave of protection enveloped his body. At once he felt a kinship, as if through osmosis or diffusion, with the deceased Gunther and the peculiarities of Mark Rose...a man he never met, and with each passing moment the sensation seemed less mystifying. He picked up the small container and removed its stringed contents. Hand knew what to expect, he'd seen the brown wrinkled forms before throwing them to the wall. Now he felt as if he were being beckoned into a secret fraternity, and it was a feeling of safety.

The ears, fingers, and tongues uncoiled from the box as Hand heard himself humming the big band tune "A String of Pearls." He remembered the first toy gun his father had given him, and how he felt powerful just turning it over in his grasp. Automatically, he felt himself move from the world he'd once known to a separate reality, one that was shared by the likes of Gunther and Uncle Bill. It was so odd…the world's strangest transformation…not bad, but unstoppable as well as revealing. The fear he'd once felt from his wild emotions now seemed to have a place, and the unseen cata-lyst for the journey became clearer with each second. The chaotic impulses that had been so mystifying since the shooting were now taking on a specific order; there was a resigned acceptance of events that simultaneously allowed recognition of where he was going and where they might take him. It wasn't uncertainty anymore as much as a transfer of energy and knowledge.

He would not be returning to the world that had been his for the last thirty-three years. His would become the emotional con-nection with the haunted spirits that still stalked the Viet Nam jungle…those lone soldiers condemned to walk the landscape in quiet desperation. On eternal patrol. Civilians that were used as killers in Viet Nam, now struggling in their quiet worlds…worlds that were closed to all who didn't share their experience. Hand embraced their collective identities and at the same time under-stood what forced them to never return to the land they had left. He was being swept away, rising on the imaginary wind that car-ried him over hills and across valleys to the point of no return, and the acceptance of his newfound relationship to himself and every-thing around him. The soft warmth of realization had a soothing effect. For the first time since the shooting, he began to relax. For the first time, he began to understand and accept that the place he was being transported to wasn't bad…just different. It was only scary if you allowed yourself to be caught in the netherworlds of in-betweens. Not really purgatory, not between worlds, but tele-ported to another reality. He could begin to formulate a condition wherein he would be at peace with the "new" Dick Hand, and forever turn loose the "old" one.

As he turned the collection of rubbery ears and tongues, he

caught himself smiling an unknown grin...a solitary secret. He now knew he could not reveal nor could he ever rid himself of the involuntary changes that had occurred in the backyard of a Vancouver house. Much of himself seemed as distant as the furthest stars, but there was an inner peace that he now knew existed only for those men who by chance had found themselves in shoes like his. It affected everyone differently, he knew that, but for Dick Hand, the passing esoteric conceptualizing of PTSD no longer was remote. He remembered Kipling's poem...his favorite, but one he'd not recalled until this very moment: "If you can keep your head when all about you..."

Then, in one of those great thundering jolts in which a man's real motives are revealed to him, Hand jumped to his feet and understood exactly what had occurred and how simple all the world had become.

Gunther's exit, and the voluntary taking of Rose with him, was an act of love. In combat with a Marine Corps grunt company, you were the closest family in existence. Closer to anyone you'd ever know before or after. Brothers to the end...a bond Hand hadn't understood just days ago, and by the odd quirk of fate in Vancouver, he'd now entered the warriors' world...one he could never leave. He now understood that Gunther and Rose had to be with those men again, it was a love that united these comrades in life and death. The journey to Valhalla, to sit at the side of the Valkyrie and wait with them there...to be called again when heroes were needed...when valor and love would again be synonymous. Spirits of long-ago fallen soldiers who, in Wagner's credo, sat patiently, anticipating the signal to be heralded back into the present-day world. Warriors, not really dead, but temporarily sidelined. Spirit personalities who awaited the call to arms, the final struggle, one that Friedrich Nietzsche knew was inevitable and would usher in the ultimate challenge between good and evil. He suddenly knew why Gunther did what he did on that long-ago day in Viet Nam. It was an act of love. Love for his men...a love so great that Rose had to be sacrificed for the greater cause. He was now certain that both Rose and Gunther had that very discussion before they left this world for the next. They understood. They were at peace. Of that Hand was sure.

He left his wife a note: *Going to see Bill, don't worry*. It wasn't signed.

The trip north to Laguna took forty-five minutes. He paid special attention to the troop movement on Camp Pendleton. The benign call of warriors seemed to emit from the hills. It was powerful, why had he never felt it before? He'd passed the huge Marine base many times over the last twenty years, even surfed at the northern end of the property with friends in high school. Now the encampment seemed to beckon him; just to turn and enter the land would make him feel safe and comfortable. But he knew he had an appointment with his uncle. The string of parts he wore around his neck whispered the truth. There would be no turning back.

He pulled into the driveway of his uncle's condo and turned off the engine. Sitting behind the wheel, he tried to collect his thoughts and at first realized that he wasn't sure what he'd be saying or sharing with Bill. The collection of body parts was tucked under his shirt, and he loosened the buttons so as to disguise his necklace. Hand slowly walked to the door and knocked. No answer. Through the heavy screen metal he could see that the wooden door to the deck was open, so he knocked harder.

"Come on in, it's open." Hand recognized his uncle's voice. "I'm outside, grab a beer, we need to talk."

Hand went to the kitchen, got a Coors from the refrigerator and went out on Bill's balcony overlooking the ocean. His uncle was seated at the same table where they'd hashed out the mystery of the Rose killings. His back was turned to Hand and he motioned him to sit without saying a word.

"You were right," Hand said. "Follow the ears and you'll solve the case. What I didn't know was where the case would *really* take me...you could have told me that, but I guess I had to find out on my own. Got any thoughts?"

"I've been reading the newspapers, you're quite the hero. A real dead-eye," his uncle smirked, but did not answer his nephew's question. "You taught both those guys a lesson, didn't you Dicky boy?"

"I'm not sure who was taught the lesson, Bill, a lot of things happened, and for me, they just continue to happen. I'm on a ride that I can't get off of, a roller coaster that's been going up and down ever since the shooting. I'm on a weird trip, that's for sure, and really felt like you were the only one I could talk to about any of this. Do you get my drift?"

"That depends on how far you've come...really where you've changed, how your world has changed. Traumatic things change people in different ways, so what I have to say to you depends on who you are now compared to who you were before. Get the point?"

Hand turned and stood up. With a nod of understanding to what his uncle had just said, he opened his shirt to display his necklace of ears, tongues, and fingers. Bill looked briefly at the parts, then his eyes lifted to meet his nephew's. Words were not needed, and nothing that could be said would add anything to the answers. "This far," Hand stated.

Bill stood and opened his shirt, revealing his own necklace. "Welcome home, Detective Hand."

LaVergne, TN USA
24 September 2009
158848LV00001B/12/P